Amanda Boulter lives with her partner and two children and teaches English and creative writing at King Alfred's College in Winchester.

Around the Houses

Amanda Boulter

Library of Congress Catalog Card Number: 2001092085

A complete catalogue record for this book can be
obtained from the British Library on request

The right of Amanda Boulter to be identified as the
author of this work has been asserted by her in
accordance with the Copyright, Designs and Patents Act 1988

First published in 2002 by Serpent's Tail,
4 Blackstock Mews, London N4 2BT
website: www.serpentstail.com

Printed by Mackays of Chatham, plc
10 9 8 7 6 5 4 3 2 1

For Ruth, Isaac and Sam

ACKNOWLEDGEMENTS

Thanks to Steven Cerretti, Helen Boulter and my colleague, Andy Melrose, for encouraging my writing and for their advice about the manuscript. Thanks to my parents Jackie and Ralph Boulter for their love and support, to my sister Sally Woods, and to Siân Jones, Corinne Marsh and Marie Beale for their friendship and for reading drafts. My deepest thanks are for Ruth Gilbert. Thank you, Ruth, for inspiring me, for supporting me, and for being so insightful and funny. This book is for you.

Chapter 1

Burnt Offerings

'Anna, what the hell are you doing? Why are you in the dark?' Cass stumbled into the bathroom, hitching up her pyjama bottoms. 'I thought you were having a pee.'

Anna was standing on the toilet seat, leaning out of the frosted window. She turned around.

'Shush! They'll hear you.'

'Who? What are you talking about?'

'Not so loud! It's next door. I've been watching them.' She poked her head back out of the window.

'Anna, it's five o'clock in the fucking morning!'

'I know and they're out there on the patio. Something strange is going on.'

'Oh God! I'm going back to bed.'

Anna grabbed her by the arm. 'You can't leave now Cass, you're a witness.'

'Am I fuck! I'm off!'

'But what if they do something, and I'm here by myself, a pregnant woman!'

'Don't even try it!'

Anna grinned. 'But anything could happen to me.'

Cass smiled back. 'Really? And I wonder what the midwife would say if she heard about you standing on a toilet in the middle of the night, nosing at the neighbours?'

'You wouldn't dare!'

'Oh yes I would! And she'll go on and on and on, boring the tits off you about being sensible and doing things safely and not getting—'

'Okay! You win!' Anna eased herself down from the window. 'You're such a fucking smart-arse sometimes.'

Cass slapped her on the bum. 'Smart-arsed enough to get my girlfriend pregnant!'

'Very funny!' Anna sat on the loo. 'And what about next-door?'

'What about them?'

'I told you! There's something weird going on!'

'Well they are weird. Can't we just leave them to it?'

'No way! You have a look!'

'What?'

'Go on, please. Just a quick one.'

'No!'

'Puh-lease!'

'Oh all right!' Cass squeezed her foot between Anna's legs and pulled herself up to the window. She jumped down again.

'Well?'

'They're having a barbecue.'

'No?'

'Yes.'

'What are they cooking?'

'I don't bloody know! And as long as it's not the cat, I don't give a shit. Now, I'm going back to bed. Are you coming?'

'I'll be one minute.' Anna watched her go.

Next-door, seventeen caged rabbits were watching from the shed as Ida and Sidney Prestwick prepared for the ritual burnings. Sidney was on his knees cleaning the crazy paving with a toothbrush while Ida shone her torch into the cracks. She nodded.

'You've done well, Sidney. The Wise Ones will be pleased.'

She switched off the torch and clipped it to her flameproof housecoat. The day was dawning over the South London skyline. It was almost time for the sacrifices.

Ida found two grips in her pocket and skewered her dangling hair into place. Her tinted curls were more urine-yellow than honey-blonde, but they still drove Sidney wild. They had to watch for his passions, especially after last year. In his excitement he had leapt naked across the sacred flames and caught the end of his beard on a hot log. The smell of singed hair still turned Ida's stomach. This year they had taken precautions. They were performing the ritual burnings on a barbecue and Sidney's remaining whiskers were tucked up neatly in a Femidom.

At her feet Ida had a large black box covered with chalk markings. It held all the offerings she had collected from the four neighbouring houses. By sacrificially burning something from these households (the more intimate the better), she and Sidney were symbolically cleansing their sacred site of the pollution from the houses on top of it. Sidney began the chant. At first it was a low murmuring, as if he were clearing his throat, but soon the rumble of numbers became audible. 'Ninety-six, ninety-seven, ninety-eight, ninety-nine, a hundred; ninety-six, ninety-seven, ninety-eight, ninety-nine, a hundred.' Ida began to sing.

Next door Anna recognised the tune of 'London's Burning', but something was different about it. She craned her neck out of the window, trying to make out the words.

> Praise the Wise Ones, praise the Wise Ones,
> In space ships, in space ships,
> You crashed, crashed here,
> You are under this old chunder.

Ida held up a bundle of screwed-up newspaper and placed it on the barbecue. It spat and sizzled in the flames and Anna winced as the smell hit her. Burnt vomit. Sidney stood over it chanting. 'Ninety-seven, ninety-seven, ninety-seven.' Then Ida began to sing again.

> *All the houses, all the houses,*
> *Built on you, built on you,*
> *They're shrines, they're shrines,*
> *To the life forms under their lawns.*

Anna stretched forward to see what Ida had in her hand. It was too small to make out clearly, but there was a nasty smell of burning rubber when it hit the charcoal. Sidney started his chant. 'A hundred, a hundred, a hundred.' Anna realised with a grimace that the rubber smell was exactly that, a rubber. 97 was the student house; 100 was Ruby's, her best friend. They must have been going through the dustbins. She wanted to get Cass, but couldn't leave in case she missed something. She even thought about phoning the police. Surely it was an offence to burn other people's condoms? Ida was singing again.

> *Here's the debris, here's the debris,*
> *From the dustbins, from the dustbins,*
> *Fire fire, fire fire,*
> *Purify it, burn and fry it.*

Ida held up a pair of red and yellow tights and Anna pulled back from the window.

She didn't wait to hear Sidney chanting their house number, 'Ninety-six, ninety-six, ninety-six,' but climbed down from the loo and ran to wake Cass. She dragged her bleary-eyed from her two-minute sleep.

'Honestly, I've just seen them burning those stripy tights you bought me. They must have been going through the bins.'

'Alright, I'm coming.' Cass pulled herself up to the window.

Anna prodded her from below. 'What are they burning now?'

Cass looked back in. 'I don't know, I can't tell without my lenses in. But they're doing Greg's house. Sidney's going "ninety-nine, ninety-nine, ninety-nine".'

'Let me look!' Anna grabbed the back of Cass's pyjamas and heaved herself up next to her. Their two heads just fitted through the window. Anna squinted into the early morning gloom. A small pink arm was just visible, poking through the barbecue grill. She whispered to Cass. 'Oh my God, they've burnt his Barbie!' They both started to shake with suppressed laughter. Whether it was tiredness or tension, Anna felt herself becoming hysterical. She couldn't look at Cass without splurting noisily through clasped hands. She hopped backwards off the loo.

'Shit! Do you think they heard us?'

Cass shook her head. 'They're still at it. Listen.'

They could just make out the final verse of Ida's song.

> *O rise up, O rise up,*
> *And take us, and take us,*
> *Aliens, aliens,*
> *We are waiting, for the mating.*

Anna whispered to Cass. 'Did I hear that right? Do they want to have sex with aliens?' She tried to stop the laughter. 'Cass, you've got to look!'

'Why me? You started it.'

'Because as you keep reminding me, I'm pregnant.'

'But what if they're, you know, doing it?'

'What, with aliens?'

'No. With each other.'

'Urgh, that's worse.'

'I know.'

A minute later, they were both peering over the window ledge. The patio was empty. There was no sign of Sidney or Ida, and only the rabbits hopped across the slabs. Then, with a clattering thud, the kitchen door opened and they both ran naked across the lawn. They were carrying shovels. In the centre of the lawn they dug two small holes.

Anna nudged Cass. 'You don't think they'll . . . you know, with the rabbits?'

'What?'

'Nothing.' She covered her eyes. 'I can't look.'

Cass was still watching the Prestwicks. Ida and Sidney were facing each other, holding hands. Gradually, slowly, they crouched down over the holes.

Anna prodded Cass with her elbow. 'What are they doing?'

Cass didn't answer. She just reached for the handle and pulled the window shut. Anna was peeved.

'What's happening? I didn't see!'

'Lucky you!' Cass jumped down and danced around the bathroom, waving her arms in disgust.

'What was it? What did they do that was so terrible?'

Cass grimaced. 'Let's just say that they were making their own little offering to the aliens.'

'What? Shitting on the lawn?'

'Oh yes. And take it from me, Sidney is going to need his legs washed.'

Chapter 2

Saturday Morning

'Don't be thick, Flick.'

'C'mon then, how'd Anna get pregnant?'

Ruby glanced at the clock. 7:20. Too early to be having this conversation. She'd already been woken up by Ida's dawn raid on the dustbins.

'You know how, with Andy.'

'So he shagged her!'

She groaned. 'Oh, for fuck's sake. No.'

'Bet the other chick watched.'

Out of the corner of a half-closed eye, Ruby could see her new satin sheet puckering over Flick's crotch. She thought about the cost of dry cleaning. Flick grinned at her, flashing the piercings in his mouth.

'Bet he had 'em both. Together.'

He reached for her nipple and gave it a tweak.

'My birds love all that lesbo stuff.'

Ruby propped herself up on the headboard and reached for her cigarettes.

'Believe me, I'm beginning to see the appeal.'

She looked at Flick's arm draped across her belly. A tattooed snake curled down from his elbow, its jaws wide around a hairy mole on his wrist. Two weeks ago, when they'd first met, that snake had attracted her. He'd bought her and Anna a drink in The Scala and she'd asked if the snake was eating a hedgehog. It wasn't supposed to be a chat-up line, but she was drunk and having a good time, and he was twenty-five and pierced all over. She couldn't help herself. She told him she had a hedgehog at home that only ate snakes. The joke took him a while, but she got it in the end.

And now she'd had her fill of it. Her breasts sagged around his arm like flabby batter on a deep-fried sausage. Sex with Flick had all the appeal of last week's toad-in-the hole. Except for that pierced tongue. If there were one thing she could cut off and keep in a jar it would be that. Maybe she'd just give him something to eat before she finally sent him on his way.

It was eleven o'clock when she eventually rang Anna.

'Hi, it's me. I've split up with Flick.'

'Oh, Ruby, that's a shame.'

'No, it's not. It's a relief for everyone and you know it.'

'Okay, you're right. I just didn't want to sound mean.'

'Why not?'

'Well . . .'

'You need to get mean. When I tell people you're a pregnant lesbian, they think you're some kind of brick shithouse with an extension. But you're not even a lean-to.'

'I resent that. Anyway, who've you been talking to?'

'Don't panic, nobody knows. I was being mean.'

'I hope you weren't mean to Flick.'

'I was sweetness itself. I said "Flick, I'm giving you the flick."'

'What did he say?'

'Durr, that's original.'

'Heard it before, had he?'

'It would seem so. Hold on.'

Anna could hear muffled voices, then the sound of a door slam. Ruby was back.

'Quick, look out the window. Flick's just left.'

Anna opened the bedroom curtains. 'You mean he's been there all this time?' She could see Ruby at her window, waving and pointing, in a purple kimono. Flick was standing on the pavement in front of her house. 'Oh no. He looks really upset.'

'No, he doesn't. He looks pissed off, there's a difference.'

'Well, he looks upset to me, and I can see his face. Maybe he'd really fallen for you.'

'Fallen my arse. He's just tried to get fifty quid out of me.'

'That doesn't mean it wasn't love.'

'Very funny. If you feel so sorry for him, let him squat in your bed for a fortnight.'

'No thanks.'

'Well, don't say I didn't offer. Anyway, never mind him, there's that new student. The gorgeous one.'

Across the road, a young black man was taking the cover off his motorbike.

'Ruby, Flick's not even gone yet and you're already looking for the next one.'

'I am not! I'm just being neighbourly.'

'Oh God, speaking of neighbours! You can't imagine the latest weirdness from next door.'

'I don't know if I want to.'

'They've been barbecuing rubbish in the middle of the night and shitting on their lawn.'

'What, and eating it?'

'No, Ruby! But they've been in our dustbins.'

'I know, I heard them.'

'And don't you care?'

'Not really.'

'Well, it freaks me out. What if they're putting a curse on us? What if it's all symbolic, like voodoo?'

'I doubt it somehow.'

'But you don't know. They were burning one of your condoms.'

'Well, perhaps I'm in for some hot sex.'

'Ruby, you're not taking this seriously!'

'You're right.' She was gazing down the street. 'But I am taking him seriously.'

The new student was adjusting something on his motorbike with a spanner. They both watched for a while and Ruby made approving noises about his muscle tone. Anna sighed.

'Actually, I spoke to him yesterday. His name's Johnnie and he's an old friend of Greg's.'

'Johnnie? Like in rubber johnny?' Ruby laughed. 'It's a sign. Thank you, O Sacred Barbecue!'

'That's not funny! Anyway, before you get too excited there's bad news. He's moved in with those two women from last year, and there's another one coming today.'

'Another what?'

'Girl. Are you listening to me?'

'Yes, yes.'

'No, you're not. I can see you. You're still watching him.'

'So, I can look and listen at the same time.'

'I'm saying that he's going to be living with three girls.'

'And?'

'Well, he's probably after them. The one coming today is only just eighteen.'

'Too young for him.'

'I think he said her name was Shirley or Sheila or something like that.'

'God-awful names. He'll never go for her.'

'How do you know? He might have a thing for granny names.'

'Are you saying he's a granny grabber?'

'No offence, but wouldn't that be a good thing?'

'Meaning?'

'Well, you know, the age thing. You are forty-one. It might put you in with a chance.'

'Listen, you cheeky cow, I'm a woman in my prime. Right, that's it, Lean-to Girl! I'm gonna have that man and it'll take more than Shirley-bloody-Temple to stop me.'

Chapter 3

Moving

'Harder, Shirley. Squeeze.'

'I am squeezing. It's not working.'

'Get your arms round him more. Up under his armpits.'

'I can't reach, Mum. The seat's in the way.'

Shirely's dad, who was bright red in the face and struggling for the breath to say Heimlich manoeuvre, let go of the steering wheel, grabbed Shirley's arms and pulled. She shot forward. Her head wedged itself between the window and his macramé backrest. The car drifted gently towards the HGV in the next lane.

They bounced off. Screaming. For days afterwards, Shirley relived the next few moments in slow motion replay. As they careered across the motorway, her mum closed her eyes and grabbed the wheel. Her dad hit the brakes. They skidded across the hard shoulder and shuddered to a halt, flattening a row of saplings on the grass verge. Shirley opened her eyes. Their windscreen wipers had sprouted. They flapped back and forth like leafy kebabs. Nobody said a word.

Then, without warning, her mum burst out of the car and raced around to the driver's side. She threw open the door, untangled Shirley, and hauled her dad on to the hard shoulder. He'd gone purple. Standing above him, she swung the small suitcase she called a handbag high in the air and, before he could roll away, hit him with it. He coughed in wounded surprise and a small cream pebble skipped across the tarmac.

'Honestly, Gordon, I've never seen anyone make such a fuss over a Nuttall's Minto.'

Her mum came back round to her side of the car, rearranged the bow around the neck of her blouse and got in. Shirley looked at her. There was something very unsettling about the relish she'd seen in her mother's face when wielding that handbag. They sat there in silence, waiting for her dad. Shirley watched him through the side window. She could only see one leg because he was still half under the car, but she could tell he was annoyed by the way he was twitching his foot. He'd probably sulk under there for at least ten minutes. And they were already more than half an hour late. If Shirley didn't get to the estate agents by five, she wouldn't be able to move into the house.

After exactly seven minutes they heard a shuffling noise and she saw her dad easing himself out from between the wheels. He looked up at her and she smiled back. What she really wanted to do was tap her watch and tell him to get a move on. Instead she looked away as he adjusted his trousers and got back in the car.

Her mum beamed at him. 'Better now, love?'

'Not really. Map, please, Shirley.'

Whenever her father was annoyed he always demanded a map. Shirley had thrown it down during their moment of crisis and it had slipped between some boxes. She stretched over, just reaching it with her fingertips. Her dad began shouting.

'Shirley, I said map!'

'She's looking for it, Gordon. Don't take your bad mood out on her.'

'Bad mood. Bad Mood? BAD MOOD?'

This phrase, which her dad repeated with increasing irritation, was obviously not sufficient to express his present state of mind.

'I've been out there in the middle of a bloody motorway,

having nearly choked to death on one of those bullets you call a mint, left for dead by my own wife and daughter, who both sit like Madame bloody Guillotine in the car. My life's flashing before me out there and you don't even bother to look out of the window. You just don't care about me, either of you.'

Shirley's mother tutted. 'Don't be silly, Gordy, of course we care about you. Wasn't I straight round there to save you? It's thanks to my handbag that you're still with us.'

Her mother had a firm belief in the value of a strong handbag, something with a solid handle and a profusion of pockets. Her own was a stiff-sided affair covered in a reproduction of the Bayeux tapestry. The clasp fastened securely on to Harold's eye.

Her father, clearly not pleased at having his life saved by a handbag, ignored her and started to drive. With slow determination he forced their car back on to the road and they moved off at a sedate fifty m.p.h. He wanted sympathy. Her mother patted his leg. He turned to her.

'I mean it, Pearl. What do you think it's like to nearly die like that?'

'Terrible, Gordon – I'm sure it was terrible.'

'It was terrible. Worse than terrible. One minute I'm driving along, the next minute I'm facing my maker.'

'Awful.'

'Worse than awful.'

Her mother tried again. 'Dreadful.'

'It was dreadful.'

'Worse than dreadful,' Shirley interrupted, giving her mother the map. It was a moment of humour she instantly regretted.

'Don't you get funny with me, my girl. What do you think it's like to stare death in the face? Do you think it's funny to die? I *will* die one day, you know, and you won't be laughing then.'

'No, Dad.'

He was in his stride now. He told them at length about the trauma of his near-death experience, and as he did so the story began to change. Shirley found herself sympathising with his brave struggle to save wife and child from a ten-car pile-up whilst blacking out from lack of oxygen. It was straight out of *Motorway Crash! Bang! Wallop!* on ITV. She realised he was practising the version he'd tell his drinking chums at his local, the Gun and Gibbet. Her mother kept oohing and aahing and patting his knee. She only paused briefly to rummage in her bag for another mint, which she popped neatly and meaningfully into her mouth.

Chapter 4

Madrigal Close

Anna was bored. Cass had been chatting with the midwife and they were making her stay in bed all weekend because of her blood pressure. She was feeling resentful, propped up on pillows and surrounded by horror-filled pregnancy books. She closed *Real Birth: The Things Even Your Mother Won't Tell You* and tried *Learning to Grunt: The Animal Instinct in Childbirth*. She could hear Cass downstairs making tea before she went to work. She'd wanted to stay home, but Anna had insisted she go. Saturday was the café's busiest night.

A car drew up outside and Anna leapt over to the window, hoping for a visitor. It was the new student moving in; she'd forgotten about her. She pulled back the nets and opened the window. They were all getting out of the car. First the father, greying and blazered, looking like he'd stepped off the QE2 in a high wind, and then the mother. She emerged from the passenger seat brushing crumbs off her lap, a busty woman with a breezeblock handbag. Anna felt a pang of sympathy for the mousy figure buried in boxes on the back seat.

'Well, it looks all right, I suppose, but I do wish you were in a proper hall of residence.'

Shirley said something to her mother that Anna didn't catch. She was drowned out by her father.

'We've been through this, Pearl. They don't have rooms for all of them in these London places. I still don't see why she had to come here in the first place. If she'd gone to Bournemouth like I wanted her to, she could have stayed with cousin Janet.'

'You know why she didn't go there. They didn't do the drama with the English, did they, Shirley?'

Shirley, who was getting out of the car, shook her head.

'Anyway,' the mother waved some keys at them, 'I'm going for a look round.' Ignoring the father's protests about taking boxes, she danced off up the path. He turned his attention to his daughter.

'You can give me a hand here, Shirley. I can't take everything. I don't know why you need all these toys at your age.'

'I haven't got any toys, Dad, it's only Mr H. Where's the bag he was in?'

'I've taken that bag for all the rubbish your mother leaves behind her. Now, if you're embarrassed to be seen with that thing, Shirley, then leave it here. You shouldn't have brought it in the first place.'

Anna watched as Shirley put Mr H back in the boot and stood silently by the car. She felt herself getting overly involved in the drama. It was the boredom. She wanted to lean out of the window and shout, 'Take the bloody teddy.' But she restrained herself. She could hear Cass coming up the stairs.

'Why are you up?'

Anna frowned at her. 'I'm hardly shinnying down the drain-pipe. That student's moving in. I was just being nosey.' She glanced back to see Shirley disappearing into the house, a lamp in one hand, a mauve bear in the other.

Cass came over to the window just as they heard the familiar slam of next-door's gate. Ida Prestwick was storming across the road towards the car. She was a woman who had bloomed into old age as others had wilted, and she took full advantage of her senior citizen status to terrorise the students. She kept an unrelenting vigil on their house and her whole life was dedicated to complaining about it: to the neighbours, the council, the police. Her husband Sidney was just as bad, but he was quieter. Like an aged member of ZZ Top, he would sidle up to you in the street and take exception to your dustbins. They were known to all, even the odd official, as Doris and Boris Karloff.

Cass cheered her on. 'This should be fun.'

'How can you say that? I can't even look at her after last night.'

Ida was wearing the same coat she always wore, in fact, whatever the weather, Anna had never seen her in the street without it. It was a mottled mustard and brown tweed, cut to just below the knee. Cass said that Ida had stolen it from Councillor Redjep during charity bingo at Balham day centre, but Anna wasn't sure she believed her. Not that Doris wasn't capable of it. There was clearly something deranged about the Karloffs. Even before last night, Anna had always thought they were creepy. She could never work out how they had managed to find out the birthdays of every person in the Close, but they had, and on that day a card would summon the soul in question to the house of horrors for a slice of cake. Christmas was worse. Everyone was lured there for a festive bite and seasonal cheer. It was always dreadful, but the next year they all went just the same.

They each had their different reasons for accepting the invitation. Greg, who lived opposite with his four-year-old daughter, remembered Doris from when he was a boy growing up here. He still had old-fashioned ideas about Balham's community and neighbourliness and didn't want things to change. Anna went because she couldn't say no. She had, in the past, felt sorry for Doris being so odd, and didn't want to hurt her feelings. She dragged Cass along with her for moral support. Ruby went for the sheer hell of it. She was always up for a night with the Karloffs. They amused her. Last year she had tried to teach them the Timewarp from *The Rocky Horror Show*, 'That's it, Sidney, you take a jump to the left.'

Even the students sometimes came, depending on how involved they were in the Close. They called it the Close, although officially it was part of Madrigal Road. Nos. 96–100 to be precise. The houses were set apart from the rest of the street because the road suddenly veered to the left, like a foot on the end of a leg. Anna always thought that some nineteenth-century builder must have got his measurements wrong and had to add on five houses in the next field. Doris obviously thought they were sitting on an alien invasion. Anna lived with Cass in no. 96, a very ordinary brick semi with a bay window and stained-glass door.

The Prestwicks were in no. 98 and seemed to make it their mission in life to police the state of Anna's front garden. Their own was concrete and filled almost to bursting with plastic urns and ornaments. This, as Doris told her, was to show them all what a neat and well-kept garden should look like. She said it showed respect. The only house the Karloffs did approve of was Greg's across the road, no. 99, which his parents had improved when they were alive by covering it in pink and grey stone cladding. Greg kept promising to change it, but Anna knew that he never would. He was next to the student house, no. 97, and both of these were in their own ways unpleasant viewing. The rented house had that lonely look houses get when they are full of people whose real home is always elsewhere.

On the corner, no. 100, Ruby's house, blazed like an outlandish full stop on the end of an ungrammatical street. She had painted the front of the house in wavy blue and terracotta stripes. Or rather she had allowed one of her many young lovers, fresh from an Arts Foundation, and very influenced by Argentinian design, to paint it for her. She had no real interest herself, but knew that it would infuriate Doris, and that was reward enough. Her attitude was that as a single woman in her forties it was her duty to resist the bland temptations of magnolia. From walls to knickers, everything would be colourful.

Doris was giving Shirley's father her neighbourhood watch speech. They could only catch snippets.

' . . . happy to keep my eye . . . make it my business . . . can't be too careful . . . living together . . . London . . . young people . . . phone number . . . ring if there's . . . get my book . . .'

As Doris came back across the road for her little black book, Anna decided that they must save Shirley from her clutches.

'Cass, you've got to go over there and save her. If she gets their number that girl won't have a life.'

'I'm supposed to be at work.'

'Just five minutes. Tell them you'll look out for her.'

'Do I have to?'

'Yes.'

Cass hung on the door. 'I've got to get my bike first.'

Anna blew her a kiss and turned back to the window. Cass came back over, putting her arms around her.

'Is that all the thanks I'm getting?'

She stroked Anna's hair as they kissed.

'Promise me you'll rest tonight.'

'Yes, yes. Now go on. Quick, before Doris comes out again.'

Anna watched as Cass wheeled over to the car, helmet perched on her head. She went straight for the mother, who was bending over the boot. As they stood up she could hear Cass talking.

'Yes, I can imagine it is difficult. So are you staying here tonight?'

'Gracious me no! Gordon and I are far too old to go slumming it in a student squat.'

'It's not a squat, Mum.'

The father shouted across, 'I should think not, not when I've just paid that estate agent fellah nearly eight hundred quid.'

Cass smiled at him. 'That was probably Andy. He's a good friend of mine.'

He eyed her suspiciously. 'Are you one of them too?'

'An estate agent? God, no. I work in a café.'

'Because he'd better look after my daughter after all that money I've given him.'

'Gordon, he's an estate agent. He's not there to look after Shirley.' Pearl smiled apologetically at Cass. 'A café? That sounds interesting.'

'You could come down if you stay over. We're renowned for our Sunday morning fry-ups.'

Pearl was keen. 'We love a good fry-up in our family, don't we, Gordon?'

He looked at Cass. 'I didn't think you looked like an estate agent.'

She ignored him and spoke directly to Shirley.

'If you need anything, I'm just across the road. You're welcome to come over any time.' Shirley opened her mouth but her mother was louder. She exclaimed triumphantly.

'Now did you hear that, Shirley. Isn't that nice!' She grabbed Cass's handlebar. 'Oh, that is good of you. You don't know what a comfort that is for me and her father. These young girls like Shirley don't realise what a mother goes through when she leaves her child. It's such a wrench for me to be away from her. Isn't it, Gordon?' He didn't respond. 'When we go down that motorway tomorrow I'll feel it like a physical pain.'

Gordon grunted. 'Won't we all!'

Cass turned back to Pearl. 'If you give me your number, I can always ring you if there's an emergency.'

'Oh, that's so good of you. That old lady offered, but I always feel much happier with a young person. You never know with the old ones if they're all there in the head.'

'Mother!'

'Well, it's true, Shirley. Look at old Mrs Penwitty. If I ever get like that you know what you've got to do.'

Cass caught Shirley's eye and a small smile passed between them. Over their heads Pearl was shouting across to Doris, who'd reappeared with the book. 'It's all right, thank you, dear,' she said with exaggerated slowness, 'we're giving our number to Cassandra.'

Chapter 5

The Cosmic Café

As she opened the door to the café, Shirley knew it was a terrible mistake. Her parents were going to hate it. The walls were bright orange and it was packed with the kind of people her dad called 'the dregs'. Cass was nowhere in sight. She tried to back out but it was too late. They were already pushing through the door. There was a pause as they looked around.

'Oh, I see,' said her mum, looking up to the ceiling, which was dark purple and had the solar system painted across it, ' "the Cosmic Café".'

Her dad had wandered ahead and was trapped in the crowd, jostling among trays of carrot cake and couscous. He grimaced at the line of rainbow jumpers and pony-tails queuing for the food counter. Her mother leant over.

'I think it's all a bit hairy and colourful for your father.' She smiled, watching him. 'Still, I'm sure we can make the best of it.'

She pushed Shirley forward. The moment for retreat had passed, her mother had taken control. They followed her to an empty table.

'Oh darling, look at these wonderful walls. You know, I'd have done my kitchen like this if I didn't have to live with your father.' Shirley snorted in derision. Only two months before, her mother had destroyed their kitchen completely and had it refitted in pastel yellow and country oak.

Her dad bellowed at her. 'Is that pig noise you, Shirley? Are you giving your mother cheek again?'

He leant across the table and it rocked unsteadily from side to side. 'I can't eat off this thing, Pearl. It's falling to bits.'

'Gordon, don't exaggerate. It's distressed. It used to be the fashion.'

'Distressed? I'm distressed. The table's having a bloody breakdown.' He laughed at his own joke and Shirley forced a smile. Her mother was too distracted. She'd noticed the pictures.

'Oh Shirley, Shirley, look at the paintings.'

On the back wall of the café there was an exhibition by an aspiring artist. As soon as she saw them, Pearl was out of her seat and on her way over. She bumped and excused her way to the back of the café with Shirley dragging behind. As a member of Frinley-on-Sea's Art Circle, she fancied herself as a bit of an expert. They squeezed past a table of students looking through sketches and Shirley's heart sank. The last thing she needed was for these people to hear her mother's opinions on brush stroke.

Her mum had reached the paintings. 'I *do* love gouache,' she was saying, 'it's so bold.'

She put her glasses on and suddenly went very quiet. Shirley caught up with her. The painting she was looking at, which was only six inches square, was green and red. Close up, however, it was quite clear what it represented. Shirley was horrified. Her mother was the first to speak.

'It's a man's doodah.'

As someone whose talent for embarrassment knew no bounds, her mother was obviously in top form. And enjoying herself.

'Oh, look at this one, Shirley.' She was pointing to a pink and blue canvas that featured the reclining figure of a man from waist to knees.

'Well, all I can say is they're a lot bigger than your father's.' Shirley rooted her eyes to the floor in a desperate effort not to look at her dad.

'Mind you,' her mum was over at the other wall now, closely inspecting each frame, 'it's not really what you want to look at when you're having your breakfast, is it?'

Ignoring her mother, Shirley went back to join her dad, who, she was relieved to see, was engrossed in his *Sunday Telegraph* and taking no notice of either of them. She could feel the group of students smirking and was convinced the one with the sketchpad was probably the artist. As she sat down it occurred to her that if he was the artist, then one of the others might be the model. Or perhaps they were self-portraits. Perhaps she'd been looking at the pictures while the real thing was sitting there all the time. And with her mother commenting on the size of things. She blushed just thinking about it.

'Well, Gordon. What have you ordered for us?' Her mother grabbed her dad by the Business Section.

He flinched. 'Nothing. No one's been to the table and there's no sign of a menu. It's not what I call service.'

Shirley pointed to the psychedelic blackboards around the counter. 'It's all up there. You have to go and queue up.'

'Oh well, you can do that, Shirley. What are we all having? I want the full works.' He folded his paper and rubbed his hands together. 'Bacon, a couple of kidneys and extra sausage.'

At the mention of sausage her mum winked lewdly at her, but thankfully kept quiet. Shirley ignored her.

'It's a vegetarian café, Dad.'

'Well, you can have my vegetables.'

'No, Dad, I mean they don't do meat.'

He was incredulous.

'Well, what do they eat then?' This was directed rather aggressively *en masse* to the other customers. Some of them looked round.

'Pretend meat.'

Shirley was saved from her father's loud opinions on this idiocy by her mother's intervention.

'Well, we'd better have that then. Go and order it, Shirley.'

When Shirley got back to the table her dad was muttering into his paper and her mum was cleaning the cutlery with a Wet

Wipe from her bag, a clear sign that they'd had words. As she sat there with her parents, she looked across at the art students. There were probably ten of them and their table was piled high with cigarette packets and coffee cups. They were just the kind of people who wouldn't look twice at Shirley or even know she existed. She couldn't have joined that table, even if she wasn't with her parents. They may be embarrassing, but it wasn't their fault she was on the outside looking in. She always was.

When the food arrived, Cass came with it. She seemed to know everyone in the place. Shirley smiled at her, pleased but shy. If Cass hadn't come over yesterday, she would never have dared to speak to her. Her face was dark and kind, cherubic-looking really, but without her cycle helmet on they could see that her hair was an inch long and bright pink at the tips. She also had two rings in her eyebrow and a pink triangle in her nose. Shirley was torn between total admiration and the secret feeling that Cass would look much prettier if only she'd let her hair grow. She could see her mum was thinking much the same thing.

'You made it, then. Hope you enjoy the Sunday Special. I bet it's your first time with a veggie fry-up, hey, Gordon.' She winked at him as she put the plate down.

Her dad brightened, pleased to be flirted with, even by a punk rocker, as he insisted on calling Cass later.

'Oh, I wouldn't quite say that, would you, Pearl?'

Her mum smiled as Cass handed her the other plates.

'There's no telling with you, dear.'

Cass laughed. 'Well, there's always a first time for everything,' she smiled at Shirley, 'even for you, Pearl.'

Cass went back to the counter and Shirley stared at her plate. Her mum was already tucking in, but she could see that her dad felt the same as she did. He was prodding a lump of fried white stuff with his fork.

'Is this what they call futon?'

'It's tofu, Dad. A futon's a mattress.'

Her mum looked up, mouth full. 'No, I think your father's right, Shirley. It definitely tastes like mattress.'

Shirley grimaced. 'Do we have to eat it?'

Her dad threw down his fork. 'Well, I'm not eating this rubbish. I want something normal.' Pearl hissed at him from across the table.

'No one is leaving this table until these plates are empty. Cass has offered to look after Shirley for us, Gordon, and we are not going to offend her.'

'But she's a punk rocker who eats futon.'

She pointed her knife at him. 'Listen, Gordon, when we go home today, we are leaving Shirley on her own in London. Cass has offered to be her friend. She's offered to ring us if there's anything wrong. Now pick up that fork and start eating.'

Gordon managed the bacon flavour crispies and the fried bread. Shirley ate his mushrooms, and Pearl had his tomato. They compromised on the tofu, which Pearl wrapped in a tissue and put in her handbag.

When they were finally able to go they thanked Cass and said how much they'd enjoyed it. Her dad shouted his admiration over the counter. 'Yes, Pearl will have to do some of that tofu stuff next time we have people over.' He put his arm around Shirley. 'Well, my girl, that new friend of yours seems all right for a punk rocker. And who would have known she was Dutch? No trace of an accent. I only cottoned on myself when I saw the back of her T-shirt.'

As they closed the door, Shirley looked back through the window and saw the writing on the shirt. It said DYKE POWER.

Chapter 6

Settling In

It was a relief when her parents finally left. All morning she'd been desperate for them to go and no longer cared if it showed. After her mum had declared in a loud voice that it all needed a good clean, and her dad had shouted at Tony Blair on the news, their departure was not a second too soon. Now she was alone in her room with its magnolia walls and maroon swirl carpet. All her things from home were inside the supermarket boxes on the floor. Her mum had wanted to unpack them, but Shirley had stopped her. She needed to do it herself. It was her big gesture of independence. She sat down on the bed, feeling lonely and lost, with no idea where to begin. She wanted her parents back.

This was supposed to be her room, but it didn't feel like it. She half expected someone to walk through the door at any moment and demand to know what she was doing there. Wherever she looked she saw other people's lives. Smudges of Bluetak where posters had been ripped down; a sock, thick with dust, at the back of the wardrobe; chewing-gum hard and grey at the bottom of the metal bin. She didn't see how she could ever be at home here. She picked up Mr H from the floor and sat holding him for what seemed like a long time.

But the unpacking still had to be done. Shirley had to go into college first thing for Freshers' Week, and she didn't want to live out of boxes. She decided to make a start. At least with everyone out she could put things downstairs without having to make conversation.

She looked among the boxes for the ones labelled bathroom and kitchen. Her mother was keen on labels. There was a series of sticky squares on the side of each box, a different colour for different contents. Books were green, music was yellow, ornaments were orange. She found the bathroom box (blue) and some kitchen ones (red) and put them on the landing. Her room was at the back of the house, so her door was at the top of the stairs. Jenni and Annabel were along the corridor, Jenni on the left and Annabel in the big room at the front. She hadn't really spoken to Annabel, but Jenni seemed nice when she was talking to her parents. She spelt her name with an i. Shirley wondered if she should do that. Shirli.

Downstairs, there was a lounge at the front, which was rather smoky and dull. Jenni had told Shirley's mother that nobody ever opened the curtains. Her mother had snorted at that and aired both the room and her disapproval. Johnnie's room was in the middle, below Jenni's, and the kitchen was at the back. You had to walk through the kitchen to get to the bathroom which, it had occurred to Shirley, would be horribly embarrassing if there were people in there when you wanted to go. She hadn't yet done all her toilet things. She planned to get up in the night when the others were asleep.

She piled her boxes on the kitchen table and began to unpack her wash bag. There were no shelves in the bathroom. Everything was piled on top of the cistern and around the bath. Shirley counted thirteen bottles of shampoo (most of them empty) and six dried-out bars of soap. She thought it safest to put her things on the windowsill even though the tiles were a bit mouldy. She cleared some space and scrubbed at them with bleach. What she thought were stains turned out to be a pattern of brown and orange flowers. She arranged her things neatly on one side, hiding her spot scrub behind the raspberry bubble bath.

She went back to the kitchen to finish unpacking there. The kitchen was a large room with a round table at one end and white units on the walls. These were the food cupboards. It was clear which one was hers because on the door her mum had left a label that said 'Shirley's Cupboard'. Every letter was written in a different colour felt-tip pen. Shirley peeled it off and prayed that no one else had seen it.

She put all the tins, tubs, packets and boxes on her shelves, trying to make them fit so that they didn't go over the bar dividing the space. Jenni had the other half of the cupboard. On Jenni's side there was a packet of Cup-a-Soup and some cornflakes. Shirley looked from one side to the other and started repacking.

'Hi.'

Shirley was trapped, caught with a tin of beans in each hand, putting food back in the box. She looked up. It was Johnnie, smiling at her from the doorway.

'Mum packed too much, did she? You can always put some of it in my cupboard if you like.'

'Oh, you can have it,' Shirley, flustered with embarrassment, held the beans out to him.

'It's okay, Shirley, I was joking.'

'No, no, I mean it. Have them.' She knew she was overdoing it, but couldn't stop herself talking.

'Tell you what,' he took the beans from her hands and put them back on the shelf. 'I'll cook using your stuff. What've you got in there?'

Shirley was completely beside herself. Being with Johnnie made her feel bland, white and provincial.

'Oh it's all really boring. They don't have any black people in Frinley, it's all English food.' That sounded terrible. 'Except for the take-aways. Mum spends her whole life in the Chinese Dragon.'

She gave him a weak smile. He was putting things on the table.

'How about we do something with spaghetti?'

'I've got mince in the fridge.'

He winked at her and she blushed. She didn't know what else to say, so she just burbled at him.

'My dad got it. We had a vegetarian breakfast this morning at the Cosmic Café on Balham High Street, and after that he insisted on stocking me up properly. So we all had to go to the supermarket and he bought bacon, sausages, chops and mince. I told him I could never eat it all, but he said that was all right because after that breakfast he felt like eating it all himself anyway. He had loads of bacon and most of the sausages as soon as we got back. He made Mum cook it and she couldn't find the frying pan in the box, so of course there was a huge row.'

She trailed off. Johnnie had found the mince in the fridge and had put it on the table. Stuck on the front was a black and gold address label.

Gordon and Pearl Gates
Haven Lodge
3, Bexhill Grove
Frinley-on-Sea
Hampshire

'Are you posting him the rest?'

Shirley was too aghast to realise that he was joking.

'Oh no. It's not that. It's mum. She's got a thing about labels. She probably thought someone else might eat it if it was just in the fridge. No, I didn't mean it like that, not that you'd steal it or take it or anything. She's just got a thing about labels.'

The words were coming out of her mouth all wrong.

'I mean she does labels for everything.' In her eagerness to explain she was rifling through the bin bag to find him proof.

'Look!' She put the multicoloured 'Shirley's Cupboard' next to the mince. Johnnie smiled and took the meat over to the cooker.

Shirley was still staring at her mother's label. What on earth had possessed her to show it to him? She screwed it up, made some excuse about going to the bathroom, and flushed it down the loo. But it just bobbed about on the water so she had to fish it out and put it in the bin. She looked at her reflection in the mirror. She was pink, blotchy and red-eyed. She splashed herself with cold water to disguise the tears.

In the kitchen Johnnie had put some music on, something loud that she didn't recognise. She opened the door. He was chopping onions and his eyes were streaming. He looked up as she came in.

'They always make me cry, onions and *Animal Hospital*. How about you?'

He felt sorry for her. She guessed that her mother had told him she had been on *Animal Hospital* with Henry the rabbit. She usually managed to mention it.

'I cry at everything.' She was trying to be light but it didn't come out that way. Johnnie changed the subject by pointing to the CD player.

'Hendrix. I love this track. My old man calls him the black face of white man's rock. But then he's a bit of a purist when it comes to his music.'

She nodded, trying to look like she knew what he was talking about and hoping that he wouldn't ask her anything. But he didn't have the chance. Jenni and Annabel burst into the kitchen, dumping half a dozen bags on to the table in front of Shirley. Jenni sat down next to her and asked how she was doing. Annabel walked straight over to Johnnie and draped herself over his shoulders.

'Good God, Johnnie, you're cooking. What's the occasion?'

'It's for Shirley.'

'Ooh,' she drew out the sound, 'how positively sweet.' She looked at Shirley, who smiled shyly back. Annabel ignored her. 'I'm upset now. I want you to cook for me. We didn't get a meal when we let you move in, did we, Jenni?'

Jenni shook her head.

'Anyway, I'll forgive you. Guess where we've been. No, don't bother, you won't get it. Tooting's Treasure Trove Market. Jenni made me go, I didn't want to. I thought it was going to be the naffest place on earth. But it was absolutely fabulous, better than

Camden even. Well, nearly as good. And we got everyone a present.' Her voice became teasing and high. 'I've got a little something in here for you, Johnnie, something you're going to love.'

She gave Johnnie a bag which had 'Really Bazaar' spelt out in naked women. She was laughing as she gave it to him and when he saw it he backed away in mock horror. Shirley tried to join in the joke. 'There'd be uproar if we had a shop like that in Frinley.'

Jenni smiled, but the others didn't hear Shirley. Annabel was laughing with Johnnie.

'It's a little momento. We thought you might like something "really bazaar" to remind you of Miss Really Bizarre herself. Mind you, nothing on her stall is anywhere near as weird as the woman in person. Why you go for these mad old cows I'll never know, especially when you've got a houseful of nubile young beauties like us.'

Shirley could feel herself blushing as she tried to laugh along. She'd never met anyone like Annabel, at least not in Frinley, and not to talk to. She was everything Shirley wanted to be.

'Come on. We're only teasing you. Open it!'

Johnnie pulled a T-shirt from the bag. It was tie-dyed orange, green and purple, with 'Are you experienced?' across it.

He was clearly impressed. 'I love it.' He hugged Annabel and she held his face to kiss him.

'What do you think, Shirley?' For the first time Annabel looked directly at her. 'Are you experienced?'

Shirley was smiling inanely, desperate to say the right thing. She glanced over at Johnnie, who was stirring the mince. He spoke without looking up. 'It's the name of a Hendrix album, Shirley. I'll play it for you later.'

Annabel winked at Jenni, and Shirley felt crushed. She'd never be friends with them. They were getting their bags together to go upstairs.

'We're off to the Fridge tonight. Why don't you come, Johnnie?'

He looked at Shirley. 'Do you want to go?'

She felt too shy to say yes. 'No thanks.'

'Please yourselves.' Annabel was going up the hall. Johnnie sat in her empty seat.

'There's a party soon at Greg's next door, I'll take you to that if you like, Shirley.'

Annabel came straight back. 'Is there a party that I don't know about?'

Johnnie laughed her off. 'Not your sort of thing at all, Annabel. It's for his daughter.'

'Oh, you're taking Shirley to a kiddie party.' She leant over the table. 'If I were you, Shirl, I'd slap him for that. You're not that young, are you?' She grinned and Shirley smiled back.

'No, I'm eighteen. I've got my feet under the grown-up table.'

Annabel looked puzzled. 'Yeah, whatever. Come on, Jen, I want to try on your DMs for tonight.'

Shirley was still trying to explain but Annabel was already leaving. 'That's what my Auntie Janet says when it's her birthday. Mum says it's the drink talking . . .' She trailed off. Annabel was shouting from the hall.

'Don't wait up.'

Jenni shut the kitchen door behind them. 'Bye, enjoy your meal.'

Chapter 7

The Bookshop

Anna's key always got stuck in the damn lock. She hated this moment. The alarm was whining, the seconds were ticking away, and she was breaking her nails trying to get the key out. She gave up on it. There was just time for a breathless sprint across the boxes and books on the shop floor to get to the back wall and tap in the code. She hated that alarm.

She went back to the door. The key-ring that Cass had bought her was still dangling from the lock. Tinky-Winky looking forlorn and clutching his bag. This was not the way she wanted to begin the day. She was hoping for tranquillity, a chance to absorb the atmosphere of the shop and get herself together before telling them all her big news.

She loved this shop. She loved the musty smell and the old-fashioned feel of it. The way the dark wood shelves were so packed with books that they spilled on to the floor. It felt like what it was, a shop that had begun as a back-room business and taken over the whole house. In the years that she'd been working there, Anna had deliberately worked her way down through the floors of the shop to end up where she wanted to be, in the basement. In second-hand and antique books, surrounded by the past. New books were just paper, but old books had other stories to tell. The dedications, the scribbles and notes that people long since dead had once written in the margins. That was what she loved.

There was only one thing wrong with this otherwise perfect job. She was now working with Felicity Granger, the manageress. Felicity represented what was left of the husband and wife team who used to run the shop. Mr Granger had died four years ago in a shooting accident (there were those who said suicide but there was no proof. If he'd left a note she'd got to it first). She was the kind of woman who was totally unaware of the most important social changes of the last thirty years. Like the shop itself, she had entirely escaped modernisation. But in her this out-datedness was not nearly so attractive. She bore a striking resemblance to Ann Widdecome, and had none of the old building's charm.

Mrs Granger was the reason that Anna had waited so long before telling them all she was pregnant. Being an unmarried mother and asking Felicity Granger for maternity leave was not going to be fun. But then there's only so much an ethnic print smock and an overly large lunchbox can hide.

She was going to tell them today when they were all together. It would get it over with and avoid having to go through the same questions and potential awkwardness with every one of them individually. At least this way she could ruin the gossip. She knew they had their suspicions. Betty from upstairs was always giving her the eye. So today was the day, a perfect opportunity. It was the third Wednesday in the month, which made it a staff coffee morning. These occasions were supposed to bring them together as a team, so they could talk about what books they were reading and what was selling well. But mostly they just sat in strained silence until Mrs Granger let them out.

They all came, though, dutifully turning up at eight in the morning on every third Wednesday. Mrs Granger let it be known that it would be considered very bad form not to. When Trav, who'd only been there a month, failed to show it was something of a shop scandal, especially since Mrs Granger had invited him to entertain the group with tales from his travels. Trav was a bit of an oddity for Felicity. He was in his early forties and looked and spoke like a leftover from the Peace Corps. Anna really hoped that he'd told her to stuff it. But he hadn't. He was there, the next third Wednesday, treating them to a full presentation with scenic slides: 'My Time in Thailand'. But then Trav only planned to stay in London for a few months and the job in the bookshop was perfect for him.

He was updating the maps and travel section and spent his time impressing young women with his adventures in Chile, or Sudan or Papua New Guinea, or wherever else it was they were going. And if he hadn't been there, he knew a man who had. Anna was already looking forward to the beginning of what he called his last great journey. He was going home to Australia, on his pushbike.

At least she didn't work on the same floor as Trav. He was on ground with Trevor, a middle-aged Liberal councillor who specialised in health and hobbies. Trav and Trev. Anna knew it was immature, but she couldn't help it. She and Cass thought they were the perfect couple. They had a running joke making up holidays for them in Trev's caravan. It was light relief. They weren't exactly a fun crowd in the shop. There were only two of them on each floor, her and Mrs Granger, Trav and Trev, and Betty and Jeannine on the top.

Anna felt sorry for Jeannine. She was fond of her but not in a way that would stretch to friendship. Jeannine was just so scared of life. It was as if working with books allowed her to model herself on those sad spinster librarians in 1950s films. It was an alibi for not living. And Betty she simply couldn't stand.

Betty was a friend of Mrs Granger's from their club, Conservative Ladies in Croyden (CoLiC), who, after years of party fundraising, found herself at a bit of a loose end. The elderly male committee of the local association had decided that ladies' fundraising needed a bit of a shake-up, a more dynamic face. And so Betty had been replaced by a younger model. Quite literally. Mrs Braithwaite had once appeared as February in the *Toffs and Totties* calendar 1982. Betty's old friend Felicity

Granger came to her rescue and offered her something to do in the shop. She was in the new titles section, frightening Jeannine.

Anna collected the post and went downstairs to put the chairs out. The Wednesday meetings were always held in Mrs Granger's office, even though they could barely all squeeze in. There were footsteps above as she put the kettle on. Betty put her head around the door.

'Morning, Anna dear.' Everyone was dear to Betty.

As usual she was dressed as if she was going to Ascot. Wide-brimmed hat, pink and green dress with a white belt, white handbag held stiffly on a crooked elbow. Anna attempted civility.

'Morning, Betty, you're early.'

'Well, I like to do my bit for Mrs Granger.' Although Betty had known Felicity Granger for over forty years, she made a point of never using her first name in front of the other staff. She thought that the craze for first names at work was not only common but a symptom of general moral decline. 'She has asked me to supervise the arrangements for refreshments.'

'Really?' Anna didn't know whether to be pleased or insulted. It was officially her turn. 'I've already rinsed out the mugs.'

'Oh, I think we can do better than that.'

Betty opened her vinyl Harrods carry-all to reveal six flowery porcelain mugs with decorated stands.

'What do you think of these, Anna, a little bit more appropriate for us ladies, wouldn't you say?'

Anna looked blank. 'Well, to be honest, Betty, I prefer this.' She held up her Cats Against the Bomb mug. 'Those flowery cups just aren't really me.'

'My dearest girl,' said Betty, suddenly taking Anna by the arm with a look of matronly concern on her face, 'do you know what that tells me about you?'

'Um . . . no,' Anna muttered as Betty led her to a chair. She was confused by Betty's interest in her. They usually ignored each other.

'It tells me that you do not value your femininity. You do not want to be a lady.' The last thing Anna felt like was a lecture from Betty. She decided that polite but firm was the best defence.

'Yes, well, that's because I don't want to be a lady, Betty. I want to be a woman.'

'Then, my dear, why do you insist on acting like a man?'

Anna was half aware of the others filing into the room. She caught Trav's eye and he winked back, obviously enjoying the scene.

'Look, Betty. I don't want to argue with you. We are both women, you in your way, me in mine. Let's just leave it at that, shall we?' She turned away from Trav and gave him the finger behind her back.

But Betty was not going to be put off. 'Anna, I am only saying this for your own good. I can see your situation. I'm trying to help you.'

'What situation?' As soon as she'd said this Anna knew it was a mistake. Betty pressed her face right up to her ear.

'The situation that means you'll soon be having a baby.'

Anna looked around to see if anyone had heard. This was not the way she wanted people to find out.

'My dear girl,' Betty was leading her through the shelves to the back of the shop, out of earshot. Trav had turned back to his comic. 'Did you think I didn't know? That I couldn't tell? Those dreadful dresses you wear may fool the others but not someone like me. I've known for quite a while now and I've been very worried about you, Anna.' She paused meaningfully. 'Does the father know?'

Anna hated being put on the spot like this, especially by Betty. Part of her wanted to make up wild tales of promiscuous sex just to shock her but she couldn't. She cared too much about what people thought of her, even the Bettys of this world. She just wasn't as casual as Cass. 'Yes, of course he does.' It was true after all.

'And are you still seeing him?'

'Yes.' Anna could see where this was going. 'I still see him. He's a friend of mine.'

'He's your friend, is he?' Betty sneered at the very idea. 'And is this so-called friend of yours planning to do the decent thing? Has he asked you to marry him?'

'It's not like that, Betty.' But resistance was useless.

'Anna, you are *so* naive. This is what I'm talking about. If it's not like that it's because you're not making it like that. If you don't behave like a lady, Anna, a man will not behave like a gentleman. But it's not too late, my dear. If you would only be more feminine you would have a ring on that finger in no time.'

'Betty,' Anna was irritated and exasperated, 'you don't understand. I don't want a ring on my finger.'

'Don't be silly, Anna. Of course you do. You may think that this is all very clever and feminist now, but believe me, you are simply letting this man off the hook. Before you know it, he will have sniffed out another girl, and he'll be off. Take it from me, Anna. That's what men are like. It's all sex, sex, sex with them. Grab him now or you'll be on your own with his child.'

'Betty, it's not his child. It's mine.'

'Is that what you tell him? Well, no wonder he's holding back. I bet this young man would love the chance to be a husband and father, Anna. You have no right to deprive him of what every man deserves and wants.'

Anna couldn't argue with her. She just wanted to end the conversation.

'Look, Betty, you don't know what you're talking about. You haven't even met him.' She had played right into Betty's hands.

'Exactly my point! I haven't met him, but I should. I could talk to him. I know how men think, and believe me, Anna, when it comes to marriage they are all the same. There's no reason why this child should not have a real father.'

Anna couldn't believe this was happening. It was getting ridiculous.

'Betty, honestly, there's no need for you to get involved.'

'Oh, but Anna dear, I want to help you. You might think that I am different from you but I am not. Please don't tell Felicity Granger what I'm about to tell you, it is just between ourselves. But I know what it is like to be in your situation. I have been there myself. I know everything that you are feeling. The world has not changed as much as you think.'

This was terrible. Anna didn't even like Betty. She certainly didn't want her opinions or her interference. And now this dreadful woman had told her something so private. She couldn't simply be nasty to her, now that she'd made herself so vulnerable.

'Listen, my dear,' Betty was saying, 'I have the perfect plan. Why don't you bring this young man of yours to our Christmas dinner? I will have a little word with him.'

'Honestly, Betty, I . . .' Anna's protests went unheeded.

'Now, Anna dear, do not worry. I will be totally charming. I will just point out to him what a wonderful catch you are.'

She twinkled at Anna, who smiled feebly back. Betty was sorting out her life with absolutely no idea how Anna wanted to live. She'd run a mile if she knew about her and Cass.

'He probably won't be able to make it.' She knew that was weak. She was grabbing at straws.

'Of course he will. You must persuade him. You must use your feminine charms.'

'I thought I hadn't got any.'

'Don't be petulant, Anna. Of course you have. It is a woman's true nature to be charming.' She suddenly went silent, looking at her suspiciously. 'This man does exist, doesn't he? You didn't buy his spermatozoa off the Internet, did you?'

'Of course not.' Despite herself, Anna blushed. Why could people like Betty always make her betray her own values?

'Well, if he exists I'll expect to see him there. Now don't worry, my dear, you have friends on your side.' Betty squeezed her elbow and went off to take charge of refreshments.

Anna was trapped. What could she do? If she didn't bring a man to the dinner then Betty would be triumphant and never let her forget it. Maybe it would be best just to let her think she'd sorted it all out. Maybe she could fix it so that they'd all be happy. She wouldn't have to say she was getting married, living together would be a good compromise. Then Betty would be happy. Everyone at the shop would carry on presuming what they liked about her. Life at work would be easy. Anna decided that all she had to do was persuade Andy to come as her boyfriend to the bookshop's Christmas do.

Chapter 8

The Birthday Party

Cass and Anna were watching the party from the back-room window. Outside, a group of over-excited five-year-olds were racing around the garden in search of treasure. Cass had persuaded Greg that on such an unseasonably warm October day he had to get the kids outside. And so while they were all eating jelly and cake, she had re-routed the treasure hunt into the garden. Now they were all running after Cori, who, asserting her privilege as birthday girl, had put herself in charge. There were squeals and shrieks as they reached the last of the arrows and found a little box full of sweets and trinkets. Anna watched from the window as Greg rather ineffectually tried to encourage sharing and harmony.

'I can't believe she's five. When we moved here she was just a baby. Look at her now, she's grown up so fast.' Anna knew she'd said it about a hundred times already, but she couldn't get it out of her head. She had to stop herself getting too sentimental. 'God, listen to me, five months pregnant and I already sound like a cliché.'

'Well, you know what they say, "A stitch in time saves an episiotomy."'

'Ha, ha, Mrs Motto. Listen, I'm taking a hormonal trip down memory lane here, and what are you doing? Filling your face and laughing at your own jokes.'

Cass looked up from the pile of paper Barbie plates and Anna was full of love for her. 'Come here. You've got chocolate all over your chin. You know, sometimes I think you'd like to be five again.'

Cass gulped. 'God no. All those teenage years ahead, ten more years of school. No way! I'm happy how I am, thanks.' She leant over the jelly and held Anna's face in her hands. 'Right here with you.' They were kissing when Ruby came in.

'Dear me, girls, are you *trying* to corrupt those poor innocents?'

'Ruby, you're back. I thought this was the big weekend.' Ruby had told Anna all about her new young lover and how he was taking her for a romantic weekend away. It was a relief after Flick.

'Well, you know what a party animal I am. I just couldn't keep away.'

'I take it the weekend didn't go well.'

Ruby flung herself on a chair. 'It was a disaster. I just can't tell you.'

'Oh I'm sure you can.' Cass liked to tease Ruby about her dramatic sensibilities. She had once told her, much to Ruby's delight, that she was the only woman she knew who could out-flounce a drag queen.

Ruby scowled at Cass and turned to Anna, who was always her more attentive listener. 'Let's just say that when a man takes me away for a dirty weekend I do not plan on spending it with his bloody mother.'

'He took his mother with him?'

'No, his bloody mother owned the bloody hotel.' Anna and Cass laughed.

'Did he know?'

'Of course he knew. He only took me because he was getting it free.'

'You said it.' Cass was speaking through a mouthful of jelly.

Ruby made a face and turned to Anna. 'Can't you control your horrible girlfriend?' She pulled a packet of cigarettes from her bag. 'It wasn't funny. His mother insisted on sending us off with a packed lunch like we were two kids on a school trip. She was deliberately ruining it.' She lit her cigarette with her favourite Colt 45 lighter. 'That woman wouldn't let me pay for a thing. She kept patting my hand and telling me to put my money away. I wouldn't have minded, but not only was it clear to all that I was *not* a poor young thing like Richard' – she took a deep drag on the cigarette – 'It was also perfectly plain that I was several years older than she was.'

Anna laughed. 'Well, if you go for schoolboys, you've only got yourself to blame.'

Ruby began waving her hand to disperse the smoke.

'Excuse me, darling, it's hardly my fault if she got pregnant at twelve.'

'Twelve?' Anna was genuinely shocked. Ruby revised her estimate.

'Well, eighteen.'

Cass was pointing to the cigarette. 'Outside, Ruby, you know Greg hates it in the house. And what about Anna?' She shooed her through the kitchen, pushing her from behind. Ruby had to shout to Anna over her shoulder.

'Anyway, that's it for me. I'm taking a leaf out of your book, I'm through with men.'

'Yeah,' Anna laughed after her, 'course you are.'

Anna opened the window to let in some air. Greg hated smoke and Ruby knew it. With Ruby you either liked her or loathed her, but you couldn't stop her. Depending on how you looked at it, she was either a feisty free spirit who did her own thing and refused to obey the rules, or she was a selfish and inconsiderate hedonist. Anna liked her, so she gave her the benefit of the doubt. Others didn't. She could see her chatting to Greg outside, obviously charming him. He had Cori on his shoulders and she was banging her knees together, trying to make him run up and down. There was some sort of race going on. Johnnie, from across the road, was also being bounced on by a miniature maniac, and Cass was joining the fray. Johnnie had brought the girl she'd seen moving in, Shirley, and she was blowing bubbles for some of the others to catch. Anna wondered whether there was something going on between them. She seemed nice enough, if a bit quiet, but Anna had no problem with that.

Ruby came back in with a bottle as the race got going again.

'Greg seems very pleased with you. He was singing your praises.' She poured them both a glass of wine. Anna took a sip.

'That's because I got a book for him in time for Cori's birthday. It's quite sweet really, a collection of poems about the environment called *Nature's Children*. Greg thought Cori's mother might be in it.'

Ruby spluttered. 'What, that ranting eco-prat?'

'Shush, Ruby, the window's open.'

'Well, you've read her ravings on the kitchen wall. It's not exactly *Poetry Please*.'

Anna smiled despite herself. They'd all had a laugh about that poem, but she didn't want to hurt Greg's feelings. And Ruby was always so loud.

'She might be in it for all we know.'

'D'you mean to tell me you didn't look?' Ruby was exaggeratedly disappointed.

'I couldn't. It was shrink-wrapped.'

Ruby laughed. 'Oh, that's very eco-friendly.' She went over to the table and cut herself a huge slice of chocolate cake.

'I thought you were on a diet.'

'Yes, well, like I said, I'm through with men, diets and corsets.'

'You don't wear a corset.'

'Only the once. And I may have looked slim and gorgeous, but when we finally got it off, my stomach looked like tripe in a vice and I had absolutely no feeling below the waist. Where's the fun in that?'

They laughed and Anna scooped up a fingerful of icing from Ruby's plate.

'So,' Ruby's tone was tellingly casual. 'Who's Johnnie's young friend? New girlfriend?'

'I'm not sure. She's the one that's just moved in.'

Ruby stretched to see out of the window. 'She doesn't look exactly racy, does she? Definitely one of the fluffy bunny brigade.' This was Ruby's term for the sexually unadventurous. One of her worst insults.

'Ruby, don't just write her off. She might be very nice.'

'Are you trying to tell me that that woman does not have a pink fluffy bunny on her bed?'

Ruby wandered to the window.

'Yes, I am actually, she hasn't.' Anna leant back smugly. 'She's got a mauve teddy called Mr H.'

Ruby raised an eyebrow. 'And you know this because . . . ?'

Anna kicked her on the bum. 'I saw her move in.'

'Well, how do I know what you gay girls get up to?' She looked back to the garden. 'She's a bit young, though, don't you think? Not exactly Johnnie's type.'

'How do you know what his type is?' Anna looked at her suspiciously. 'And anyway, why all the interest? I thought you were off men.'

'Oh that. That was just a phase.' She gave Anna a wicked smile. 'Watch this. Shirley Temple step aside.'

She smacked her lips and bouffed her hair. Anna watched her walk back out into the garden all smiles and seduction. Within two minutes Johnnie was hers. She had managed to pry him from between the knees of a disgruntled five-year-old who she'd sent packing and they were sitting on the grass sharing a cigarette.

The doorbell rang. Anna answered it to a posse of parents arriving to collect their offspring. She called Greg and he rushed in with Shirley close behind. Between grabbing coats and balloons and cake and treasure and stuffing it all into little bags, Anna told him how wonderful Cori was and how much she loved her. Greg gave her a tired and emotional hug.

'You will be all right with all the mess, won't you? I feel terrible just leaving it.'

'Anna, go home! Shirley's here with me.' He put his arm around Shirley, who blushed scarlet. 'And there's always Ruby and Johnnie.'

Anna smiled. 'Oh yes, I'd forgotten about them all alone together in the garden.'

He winked knowingly. 'Don't worry, I've just sent Cori to read them a story.'

Chapter 9

Washing Up

Shirley was only trying to be polite and do the right thing. Now she found herself alone in the kitchen with Greg. She wondered if she could leave without it looking bad.

'Do you want to wash or dry? Of course, you don't have to do either. You could just chat to me if you want.'

The very idea of just chatting sent Shirley into spasm. She'd spent all afternoon surrounded by five-year-old girls who were all clearly in love with Greg, and she felt like one of them. Her eyes raced around the kitchen looking for a tea towel. She saw one on top of a pile of old newspapers in the corner and picked it up, trying not to notice the smell.

'I'll dry.' She smiled, hoping that she didn't look as awkward as she felt.

Greg grimaced. 'Oh, you can't use that. I'll get you a better one.' He pulled at the drawer under the drainer and gave her a clean cloth, taking the old one from her hand. 'It's all a bit of a mess, I'm afraid.'

He turned back to the drawer, struggling to push it shut. 'To look at this house, you'd never guess I was a chippy.'

Shirley leant against the kitchen table, imagining him behind a hot fat fryer.

'My Granny used to have a chip shop.'

Greg smiled at the confusion. 'Right.'

'And she's got an old table just like this one in her kitchen too.'

'Shirley, are you trying to make me feel middle-aged, or what?'

He was teasing her, but Shirley took it to heart. 'Sorry, I didn't mean that you were old.' She tried to say something nice. 'Cori enjoyed the party.'

'Yes.'

The sounds of dishes and running water made her even more aware of their silence. She stared at the formica desperate for something to say.

'It's an unusual name, Cori. Is it short for anything?'

'Coriander.'

'Oh.' She'd heard the name before. 'Isn't that a vegetable?'

Shirley was cringing before the words were out, but Greg didn't seem to notice. He was upbeat.

'No, it's a spice. She was the original Spice Girl.'

She laughed at his joke and he smiled too. He wanted to tell her about Coriander. What a great child she was and how he loved her.

'Coriander was the name her mother gave her. If it had been left to me I'd have probably chosen something really dull and bourgeois, like . . . well, I don't know what like.'

'Shirley,' thought Shirley, but she didn't say it. She just stared at her cloth.

'Cori's mother was a really artistic woman, you see, a poet. When I knew her she used to describe herself as a poetestor. Like protestor and poetess together. She was clever like that.' Shirley nodded, still not looking up. Greg was in his own world. 'She was a word-warrior, like an eco-warrior except she wrote poems rather than climb trees. We met at Twyford Down.' He glanced at Shirley and realised that she'd never heard of it. 'There was a protest against the M3 being built through the downs. You've probably driven through the very spot where we met. I do myself now. Funny how life goes, isn't it?' Greg pointed to an old poster on the wall above the cooker. There was a photograph of a group of people sitting on an earthmover and a poem underneath:

> *The Man raises his sword*
> *To slash the Mother's body.*
> *The Man raises his sword*
> *To fuck the Womban's body.*
> *The Man raises his sword*
> *To smash Nature's body.*
> *But our blood is the source of Life*
> *And the Man with his great knife*
> *Or the rapist with his sword*
> *Cannot silence the Womban's word.*
> *SEIZE THE POWER – JOIN US –*
> *JOIN THE MOTHER AT TWYFORD DOWN*

'That's her stuff. Johnnie tells me you're an English student so you probably know more about these things than me.'

'Not really, I'm only just starting my first year at Southside Uni.'

Shirley hated it when this happened. As soon as anyone knew she was doing English they presumed that she knew everything from Shakespeare to Jackie Collins. Well, she did know Jackie Collins because she read her mum's. But that was it. She didn't know anything else. She studied the poem and tried to look intelligent.

'Is it true? Did they use swords at protests?'

Greg laughed. 'You're worse than me.' Seeing Shirley's face crumble he wished he hadn't said that.

'I mean it had to be explained to me too. The sword is a metaphor for the violence of the patriarchy. That's what Acorn's poetry was all about – well, all the ones she read to me.' He gave a wry smile remembering.

'When she found out she was pregnant she freaked out. She just wanted to be free. The Newbury Bypass was happening then, and Manchester Airport. They were good times. But I wanted the baby, so we made an agreement. She gave me a new life and I gave her her freedom.' He paused, staring at the plate he was holding. 'She was an amazing woman. She taught me that giving birth to Cori was like planting a seed. She didn't need to see it grow just because she'd planted it. That's why she called the baby Coriander. Because she was only one of Nature's many growing things that needed the protection of her poetry.'

'I've never thought of babies being like plants,' said Shirley, rather obviously. 'Will she come back?'

'I don't know. She said she wouldn't. Well, she left me a poem that said she wouldn't.' He recited it from memory.

> *When a womban's given from her womb*
> *There is no room*
> *For the man.*
> *She's given him the greatest gift*
> *Now there's a rift*
> *They cannot span.*

'I haven't seen her since Cori was six weeks old.'

He was lost in his own thoughts. Shirley thought she should say something. She wanted to touch him. Acorn sounded like a right cow. Greg smiled, seeing what she was thinking. Or at least some of it.

'That book I got for Cori, did you see it? Acorn's got three poems in there. I knew she'd make it. She's going to be famous. I always knew she could do it. So you see, it's how it should be. I didn't have her vision. I couldn't get beyond the small things. I suppose I'm a bit of a homebody really. I'm happy if I'm just with Cori.'

Shirley reached for the plate he'd been holding just as he put it back into the sink for the third time.

He realised what was happening and laughed out loud. 'Oh, you want the plate. How many times have I washed that one? You must think I'm a right boring old dad. I bet you can't wait to get back to your friends and go to a real party somewhere.'

Shirley was too smitten to speak. She just shook her head imperceptibly and concentrated on drying up. The plate was a plastic one decorated with little pictures of Postman Pat. She put it on the table and looked again at Acorn's poster. This time she was smiling.

Chapter 10

The Father

Andy's flat was the type of place he'd describe at work as a well-designed character apartment with many original features. Translated, this meant that a beautiful old house had been roughly divided into quarters and Andy had got the front two rooms and the hall. When the flats came on to the market, his firm did the valuation. His boss didn't reckon much to the conversion plans, but Andy could see the potential. He made a deal with the builder and bought his part of the house before it was finished. He did the rest himself. A couple of partition walls and a door in the right place transformed the old drawing room and dining room into a one-bedroom flat with a courtyard garden to the side. It was through those walls that Andy met Greg (No Building Job Too Small), and it was through Greg that he met Cass and Anna. Now they were having a baby together.

When the girls arrived, Andy was just laying the table. He was pleased with himself. He'd rushed out in his lunch hour and gathered all the baby-related catalogues he could find: Boots, Mothercare, Heal's, Baby Gap. He was indiscriminate. If it had kids in it, he got it. Apart from Harvey Nic's Christmas Hampers, that was a little something for himself.

He was at his absolute campest in Mothercare and only got worse when the assistant didn't cope well. The look of disapproval on her face as he walked over to the counter was, if she only knew it, poor dear, like a red rag to a bull. He had two uses for camp: one was social, the other was self-preservation. He used camp as a weapon against those people whose faces said you should feel bad about who you are. This was the let's-see-who's-embarrassed-first-and-it-ain't-going-to-be-me camp.

After Andy had insisted that he would buy nothing unless it was a) pink and b) frilly, the assistant was moved to ask whether he was sure this baby was going to be a girl. He turned to her with as much panache as could be got out of a Hush Puppy loafer and, staring her right in the eye, replied, 'Darling, this child is going to be a queen.' He took his catalogue and flounced off just as her 'Oh how sweet' smile was fading into an 'Oh my God' comprehension.

He arranged the catalogues as a centrepiece on the table. The dinner was a mere excuse for a night of nursery fun. They'd reached the most exciting phase of the pregnancy – shopping. And the dinner was going to have to be take-away because he'd spent all evening faffing about making little pram-shaped place markers for him and his guests.

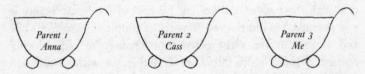

He wanted to have a little second nursery at his flat, but had been talked out of this on the grounds that he didn't have the room and he couldn't breastfeed. Instead, Andy had asked Greg to build a special cupboard in the alcove of his lounge that when pulled out would reveal toddler heaven: little table, toy boxes, drawing boards, built-in car ramps, and puppet theatre with paintings to match. He'd already designed it all and it was much more in keeping with his flat, which, contrary to what he would have people believe, especially in his office, was not all red velvet and gold lamé. It was really rather understated.

The lounge centred around three objects – an old wood burner, a huge dark green sofa and an Edwardian upright piano which still had its original candlesticks, and was one of Andy's proudest possessions. He didn't believe in carpet but had over-lapping rugs on polished floorboards. Rugs were a weakness of his and every time he went anywhere exotic he bought more. Anna and Cass loved coming here. Compared to their more ordinary house, Andy's flat had the flavour of a romantic movie. They spent hours drinking wine in the little garden, looking across the through route to glimpse Clapham Common.

Guests and food arrived together, which they all decided was the perfect start for a couch-potato shopping night. Andy flapped round Anna, saying how radiant and marvellous she looked. Then he flapped round Cass saying the same things so that she wouldn't feel left out. She shooed him off.

'Believe me, there's no way I'd want to be going through that. Bad back, piles and four months to go before shitting a watermelon.'

Anna lowered herself on to the sofa. 'Hey, can we not discuss my bottom problems before dinner?'

'Well, it all sounds very mystical and marvellous to me. I'm ignoring you, Cass, I think Anna's a real Earth Mother.'

'Oh well,' Cass was on to him, 'if you want Earth Mother, pop into the café when the yoga crowd's in. I'm sure they'll have you knitting your own muesli in no time.'

Anna laughed at the very idea of Andy being round the notorious yoga table. 'I thought you said they were the most miserable bunch of moaners you'd ever met.'

'They are. You try working out the bill for one pot of camo-mile tea between seven when not only do they all want to pay separately but those who had it weak want it cheaper.'

Andy winked at Anna. 'They're enough to put you off the lotus position.'

Cass grabbed the take-away bags. 'Ha ha. Yes, thank you, Andrew, that's enough of the single entendres.'

She was taking the lids of nos. 93, 108 and 120. 'Mmm, looks like a good chow mein.'

Anna called to them from the sofa. 'I can't move. Can you just put it on a plate for me? I'll have everything.'

Andy brought it over. 'Remind me, exactly how many are you eating for?'

'Ha ha, Mr Skinny.' Anna heaved herself up, 'I'm supposed to look like a space hopper.' She always felt more pregnant with Cass and Andy than anyone else. They were her family. The only people she trusted not to disapprove of her for not being married, or at least straight, before having a baby.

'Anyway,' Andy was pointing to the laid table, 'aren't you going to eat it properly after all my hard work?' His expression told her he wasn't serious, so she sat back and laughed when he brought her a place card which called her 'Parent 1'.

'It reminds me of Thunderbirds.'

They were debating whether this made any sense when the doorbell rang. Andy answered it and came back looking both sheepish and irritated.

'It's Tony. Did I mention that we were back together?'

Tony and Andy had lived together for two years until last Christmas, when Andy had discovered that he wasn't Tony's only lover. Tony had gone back to Italy, leaving Cass and Anna to pick up the pieces.

'No, you didn't. It must have slipped your mind.' Cass was even more acid when Tony came into the room. 'Tony, how nice!'

'And it's lovely to see you two beautiful ladies again.' Tony worked in an Italian restaurant in Croyden and greeted Cass in his most obsequious waiter-speak.

'And Anna, looking more radiant the more she grows.'

Anna gave him a cool smile. 'Tony. How are you?'

'Oh, so much better for seeing you both.'

Anna looked at Cass, who was sitting at the table, eating. She was glad to see that she wasn't rising to Tony's bait. Cass had a long history with Tony, who used to work at the Cosmic Café. They'd never got on. Tony had left after the collective had decided that his values weren't in accord with the ethos of the place. In other words he ate his own bacon sandwiches behind the counter, pinched the bottoms of female customers and was caught reading a copy of *Penthouse* in the toilets during Women Only night. It was all a deliberate wind-up as everybody knew that he was gay. But for Cass that only made it worse. The night Tony left, a crate of import lager went with him, but there was nothing anyone could prove so the finger-pointing remained bitter speculation.

'Excuse us a moment.' Andy was shuffling Tony out of the room. They went into his bedroom and Cass and Anna could hear the muffled sounds of an argument in progress.

'I don't believe he's back on the scene after all this time. What's Andy doing with a moron like that?'

Cass's answer was to the point. 'Sex.' Tony, after all, was extremely good-looking, with a body most men could only dream of.

'Yeah, but it's got to be more than that.'

'Why? Andy's a man, isn't he? Testosterone frenzy, it rules them all.'

This was the side of Cass that really irritated Anna. The side that spouted the crappy feminism she had so often heard in the café. Anna had had to give up going to the Women Only events because she always got into a row with one of Cass's old mates. She and Cass had been together nearly six years but she'd never really seen eye to eye with some of her friends. Their histories were just so different. Anna had never been with a woman before she met Cass, whereas Cass had done all those truly lesbian things like being arrested at Greenham Common and squatting in Hackney. Anna loved all the stories but didn't always go along with some of Cass's opinions, especially about men.

'Cass, can we forget the sexism for a moment? I'm more bothered about Tony being back in our life.'

'Well, he's not back in my life, that's for sure.'

'What about tonight, then? Face it, Cass, if he's Andy's partner he'll be part of our family.'

'No way! There's no way I'm letting him ruin everything. I know him, Anna, he was just proving a point tonight. He'll get bored soon and leave us to mend Andy's broken heart again.'

'Not exactly a happy ending.'

'There never is with Tony.'

Andy came back in. 'Sorry about that little interlude.' He sat down next to Anna on the sofa, but really the apology was for Cass.

'Sorry for what?' Cass demanded. 'That Tony was here or that you didn't bother to tell us you were seeing him again?'

'Both.' Andy hated the way Tony acted with Cass but then she never gave him a chance either. She would never see how sweet he could be. 'I knew how you two felt about each other. I just didn't think you would ever have met again. This family and my lovers are two completely separate parts of my life.'

'Well, why was he here tonight then?'

'Because he's an idiot. He came early because I said you were coming. But I've told him how we all feel and he understands. He accepts that he is not a part of this. You won't see him again.'

'We better not.' Cass was still pissed off. 'I don't give a damn about who's in your bed, just don't expect me to deal with them.'

Anna kept quiet but she thought that both Andy and Cass were being naive. You couldn't keep the most important people in your life in separate boxes and only take them out when it suited you. Things didn't work like that. But Andy was working on Cass.

'I don't expect you to deal with them. I can deal very well with all the men in my bed, thank you.'

'Good.'

'It is good.'

'Good.'

'Good.' Andy grinned. 'Is it good for you?'

'It's very good.'

'Good.'

'Good.' They were smiling again. He was camping it up for them.

'If my chow mein has gone slimy, I'll never force it down.'

Anna laughed. 'Oh, I'm sure you'll force it somewhere.'

'Are you trying to imply, you pregnant lesbian person, that I would sodomise a Chinese take-away? I'm shocked! Why, it's against nature.' He collapsed next to Anna on the sofa. 'But then again! Cassandra pass me the spring rolls and make mine a big one. I tell you,' he waved it at Anna, 'these are not to be sniffed at.'

She slapped him off and Cass squeezed in beside them, balancing her plate on the pile of catalogues. Andy grabbed at them.

'Okay, parents, now we're all girls together, who's in the mood for shopping?'

Chapter 11

Bonfire Night

Ruby was ready to go. She stood in front of the mirror, lipstick in one hand, joint in the other, and looked herself up and down. She was wearing a short red satin dress which fell off the shoulders and plunged at the neck. It was her B-movie outfit. She always wore it when she didn't feel quite as confident as she pretended. And tonight she was a nervous wreck. She was going to be at least fifteen years older and two sizes bigger than any of the other women at this party and she felt acutely conscious of it. Her age didn't usually bother her. All her friends and lovers were younger than she was. But tonight she felt different. She felt vulnerable. She picked up the black shawl which she'd had on and off at least five times in the last half hour and draped it around her shoulders. She wanted to look good. She wanted to impress Johnnie and his friends. It didn't happen to her often, but she had completely fallen for him. And if she was reading the signs right, this could be her lucky night.

She stood at the window, took one last drag from the joint, and watched the fireworks exploding across the sky. The party was in full swing. The music had been blaring for the last couple of hours and people were spilling out of the house and on to the street. Ruby searched the crowd for Johnnie. She knew she should just go over and find him, just burst in like she usually did, but she didn't want to. When Johnnie had asked her to come over she'd thought that it was more than just a casual invitation. She'd thought he was asking her out. Perhaps she'd read too much into it. She hoped not. She was tired of making a fool of herself.

It was gone eleven when he finally came and Ruby had almost given up hope. She saw him on the pavement, lighting sparklers for a group of girls. He looked up and saw her at the window. She blew him a kiss. When he reached the house, she was already at the door.

'Wow, you look sensational'.

She smiled.

'Are you coming to the party? I've been waiting for you. I thought you'd forgotten.'

She looked at the crowds in the street. 'I don't really know if it's my kind of thing.'

'Come on.' He took her hand. 'There's a great fire in the garden, and I'll look after you all night, I promise.'

She was touched. It was a long time since anyone had been so sweet to her.

'But I'm not dressed right. They're all wearing clothes I thought I'd seen the back of years ago.'

'You look great. That lot just hop on whatever revival band-wagon comes their way.'

'Yeah, and this is a revival of the years I most want to forget.' She could hear the bitterness in her voice but Johnnie was still smiling.

'Why's that then?'

He was so nice that for a moment Ruby almost wanted to tell him. But she couldn't do it. It wouldn't be fair. She laughed it off. 'Well, could you see me strutting my stuff in a pair of hipster trousers? Listen, the way I see it, no one should have to do hotpants and platforms more than once in a lifetime.'

He laughed. Whilst they were talking he'd been leaning against the doorframe, rolling up. Now he took one drag and gave it to her. 'Can I tempt you, then, Ruby?'

Ruby was so open to temptation it was all she could do not to drag him upstairs.

'Well, I do love fireworks.'

'Watching them or making them?'

She kissed him lightly on the cheek. 'I'll tell you in the morning.'

The girls with the sparklers had obviously been watching them, and as they walked across the street, one of them called out.

'Hey, Johnnie. I didn't know your mum was coming.'

'Fuck off, Annabel.' Johnnie put his arm protectively around Ruby's shoulders. 'Ignore her, she's just trying to wind me up.'

It was just what Ruby had been dreading and there was no way she could ignore it. That just wasn't her style. She squeezed Johnnie's hand and walked over to the girl who'd shouted.

'Can I speak to you privately for a moment?'

Annabel stared at her suspiciously but Ruby was already walking down the street. Unable to resist the challenge, Annabel followed.

'About what you just said.'

Annabel tried to interrupt with excuses, obviously feeling less confident away from her friends, but Ruby stopped her.

'I'm not interested in apologies. I know you're Johnnie's friend. I just want to know if you can be trusted with a secret.'

Annabel's face blazed with drunken curiosity. 'Oh absolutely!' she said, looking over to her friends excitedly.

'You were right.' Ruby waited for her to grasp the implication. 'I *am* Johnnie's mother, well, his stepmother. We're a very unconventional family.'

'But,' Annabel clearly wanted to believe her, 'you live across the road. I've seen you.'

'Of course. I have one house for the father and another for the son. It's less messy that way. We've been hoping to get closer for some time, so naturally when you told him there was a spare room . . .' She paused dramatically. 'This is to go no further.'

'Oh no, absolutely, I won't tell a soul.'

'I'm sure you won't. Because if you do I'll know where to come looking.' She turned sharply, leaving Annabel staring after her, the sparkler fizzling out in her hand. The friends looked on in silence as she walked back to Johnnie.

'What did you say to her? She looks gobsmacked.'

'I told her she was right, that's all.' Johnnie didn't follow. 'I told her that I'm your stepmother.'

He laughed out loud. 'God, you weren't joking when you said you might make fireworks. Remind me not to mess with you.'

'Oh, that's exactly what I hope you'll do.'

He took her hand. 'Come on, mother, you're embarrassing me.'

Inside it was dark and boisterous. Stolen road lights were flashing orange and Ruby could just make out the shapes of people dancing wildly to Santana. Johnnie eased her through the crowd towards the kitchen. It was the only room with any proper light and Ruby could see Greg chatting to Johnnie's mousy friend Shirley.

'Hi, Ruby, I wondered if you'd make it. Johnnie's been looking for you.'

'Well, you know me, Greg, I wouldn't miss a chance to get my party dress on. Or off again.' She winked suggestively at Johnnie as he went outside to check the fire.

Greg laughed. Shirley blushed. He tried to introduce them, but Ruby interrupted him.

'It's all right, we've met already. You were too busy giving piggyback rides to notice what we girls were up to. Isn't that right, Shirley?' Shirley was giggly and flushed with too much wine.

'Anyway, I won't intrude. You two were all huddled up as if you were plotting something. I just hope that it doesn't involve gunpowder. I know what an anarchist you are, Greg.'

Greg tried to match Ruby's banter. 'My name's Greg not Guy.'

Ruby smiled at him, but Shirley was banging the table, hysterical with laughter. When she stopped, Greg announced that he was going.

'Well, I'd better be off. I've left Anna looking after Cori.'

Ruby looked from Greg to Shirley. He obviously had no idea how she felt about him, and she was clearly desperate. The situation needed some help. 'Oh, don't be such a party pooper. I'm sure Anna won't mind.'

'Well, I don't want to take advantage.'

'Now, Greg, you know you can take advantage of all us girls any time you like. How about you Shirley, would you mind Greg taking advantage of you?'

'No, that would be nice.' They both looked at her with disbelief.

Ruby laughed loudly. 'Well, Greg, there's an offer for you.' She could see that he was pleased, if a bit flustered. He couldn't even look at Shirley, but that was just as well because she looked mortified.

'You're trying to lead me astray, I know you, Ruby.' He was backing out of the kitchen. 'But I really can't stay any longer. You both enjoy the rest of the party, though.'

Shirley was too drunk to hide her disappointment. She crumpled miserably on to a kitchen chair. Ruby put her arm around her before following Johnnie out into the garden.

'Don't worry, Shirley, at least he'll be thinking about you tonight.'

Outside it was cold, but the fire was blazing and people were sitting around it smoking. Someone was playing a guitar and Ruby was about to make a wisecrack about scout camps when she realised how lovely it was. Johnnie was sitting on the grass waiting for her with a joint. She let him pull her down on to his lap. She put her arms around him, snuggled up and stared into the fire.

She must have closed her eyes, because when she looked again there were fewer people and the fire was much smaller. Johnnie was watching her.

'Oh my God, have I been asleep?'

'For an hour or so.'

'Oh no, you must think I'm so boring. You should have woken me.'

'I didn't want to. You looked so beautiful that I could have watched you all night.'

Ruby laughed. She really wanted Johnnie, and wanted it to be different with him, but this kind of intimacy made her uncomfortable. She couldn't handle emotional stuff, she was much better with sex. She deliberately changed the mood.

'Well, that's very romantic, but I can think of better ways of spending the night.' She kissed him, gently biting his lip. 'Let's go to your room.' She stood up and walked back into the kitchen, hoping he'd follow.

She was trying to be seductive, so when he caught her dramatically around the waist, and pulled her towards him she thought it was passion. But she was wrong. He was dragging her out of the way. A second later a queasy-looking student threw himself in front of her, grabbed the sink, and vomited all over the draining board. She grimaced.

'Thanks. Being puked on never has been my idea of foreplay.' She turned and put her arms around him. 'Let's stay out here.'

He shrugged apologetically. 'Ruby, that guy's a friend of mine, I've got to help him out. Listen, here's my key. My room's just up the hall. I'll be there in two minutes.'

She didn't know whether to be impressed or insulted. It wasn't every day she came second to vomit. She took the key, kissed him in a way that she hoped was enticing, and began pushing through the heaving and shouting to get to his room. It wasn't quite the love nest she was hoping for. The door had been kicked open and was hanging forlornly from one hinge. There was a crowd around it, jeering wildly as one of them bared his backside to those inside. She shouted over the noise.

'What's going on in there? What's happened to the door?'

The youth next to her grabbed her around the waist. 'It's the bonking room, darling! We're having an orgy!' He was trying to shock her but she wasn't in the mood to indulge him.

'So why aren't you in there then, sad boy!'

She put her head around the door. There were several couples fumbling on Johnnie's bed. One of the girls was giggling like a hyena. Ruby could see her night of passion slipping away from her. She was about to go when she recognised that laugh. It was Shirley. She was slumped in the corner, having her toes sucked by someone hairy in a Guns 'n' Roses T-shirt. She obviously thought it was hilarious. Ruby hoped she wasn't going to do something she'd regret. She even thought about rescuing her, but decided against it. Maybe she wasn't as nice as Johnnie. Maybe she didn't want to get involved. But Shirley had her own life to live and so did she. And right now that meant taking Johnnie back to her place.

Chapter 12

The Morning After

Shirley opened her eyes. It was morning and the sunlight was glaring through her curtains. She squinted painfully at the ceiling and it swam slowly into focus. Her head was throbbing and her mouth felt like it had been carpeted. She closed her eyes again and tried to think about the night before. It was the best party she'd been to and it had really helped her to make friends with Jenni and Annabel. They had all done the shopping together at the superstore. Shirley had paid, but when their loans came through they were going to give her the money. As a special surprise for them, Shirley had bought some marshmallows for the fire.

Greg had been the first to arrive. He'd brought her two bottles of his home-made wine to say thank you for helping at Cori's party. She didn't want to drink it at first, but after a few glasses of 'Fortified Parsnip' she was swigging the 'Broadbean and Elderflower' from the bottle. She snuggled into the duvet thinking about Greg.

She could smell something nasty. She sniffed. There was an overwhelming smell of cheese. She opened her eyes to see where it was coming from. There on her pillow, less than three inches from her face, a hairy toe was poking out of a grey nylon sock. She screamed and flung herself on to the floor, taking the duvet with her. There was a man in her bed. He didn't move. He was lying on his back wearing jeans and a T-shirt. When she saw who it was she cringed with embarrassment. How did he get there? She didn't remember even seeing him at the party. But then she didn't remember much other than talking with Greg.

His name was Iain and he was on her course. She'd had poetry lectures with him but they weren't friends. She didn't want to be. They'd got off to a bad start in Freshers' Week when having gone through what A levels they'd done and where they'd travelled (Shirley had only been to the Rhône valley with her parents), they got on to music. Iain was a heavy metal fan and spent over an hour telling her all about it. She was being polite to him, even though she had no interest whatsoever, until he started talking gleefully about what they did to animals and Ozzy someone who had bitten the head off a chicken on stage. She'd told him that the chicken must have been traumatised and that it was sick, and that she loved animals and didn't want to talk to him any more. After that, every time he saw her he made slurping, clucking, chomping noises. Her friend Rachel from Nuneaton called him a greb.

She stared at him in horror. She couldn't believe that Iain was in her bed. Her only comfort was that he still had all his clothes on and so did she, except for her socks. She looked at her feet. For some weird reason the nail varnish on her big toes had vanished. She was trying to work out why when she heard Jenni outside her door. She couldn't let her come in. If it got out that she had a man in her room, especially an ugly one like Iain, she'd never live it down. Annabel would have a field day.

She picked up the duvet and threw it over him, making sure his head was covered. His feet were still poking out on the pillow and she had to put Mr H over them. She made a mental note to take him to the launderette with her sheets. She threw her beanbag on top just as Jenni knocked on the door.

'Shirley, are you awake? If you're awake can you give me a

hand cleaning up? I'm on my own downstairs. Shirley, I know you're up, I can hear you moving around. Can I come in?'

Shirley opened the door a fraction and put her head around it. 'Hi.'

'Hi.' Jenni made a face, 'God, you look terrible.' Shirley smiled feebly, looking anxiously in the direction of the bed. Jenni thought she just wanted to get back there.

'Look, Shirley, I'm sorry to drag you out of bed but it's three o'clock and it's just so terrible downstairs that I can't do it on my own. I wouldn't mind but I had to deal with Doris and Boris last night. They got the police out twice.'

As Jenni was talking, it flashed through Shirley's head that if she went downstairs to help, then Iain might wake up and wander out of her room in full view of everyone. She couldn't risk it.

'What about the others? Where are they?'

'Johnnie left last night with that woman from across the road and Annabel's still in bed. There's only us. I've tried knocking but Annabel won't answer and I know she's in there because I've been hearing the noises all day.' She leant toward Shirley conspiratorially. 'She's got a man in there. And it's not Daz.'

Daz was Annabel's boyfriend.

'Oh, I see.'

'I wish I knew how she does it. I think it's time me and you got to see some action, don't you?'

Shirley laughed hastily. Out of the corner of her eye she could see that Iain had flung the duvet off the bed and was fidgeting in his sleep. For a moment Jenni looked like she might have heard something. Shirley laughed again, louder. At last Jenni went back downstairs. 'Don't be long. I'll make you some black coffee.'

Shirley shut the door. She had to get Iain out of the house without her seeing. And if she didn't go down soon Jenni would come back up. She looked out of the window. It was a fifteen-foot drop on to a concrete patio. It was no good, Jenni would hear him fall. She thought about locking him in until later, but he'd probably call for help. Then a horrible thought struck her. If Iain woke up in her room it wouldn't matter who saw him.

He'd tell everybody anyway. She needed to get him out of her room before he woke up. It was impossible.

She flapped uselessly, trying to think of a plan. Wild thoughts that were no help at all raced around her head. She was reaching a frenzy of desperation when she heard giggling on the stairs. Annabel and her mystery man were going down for a bath. She opened her door a crack and saw them snogging in the hall. They both had towels. She knew what she had to do.

As soon as she heard them in the kitchen with Jenni, Shirley ran along the corridor to Annabel's room. It was huge and filthy. A double bed was in the middle of the floor, surrounded on all sides by piles of clothes, cushions, books and mugs. It was perfect.

Shirley ran back to her room. She had to move quickly. She grabbed the handles of her mattress and with her foot against the base, heaved it towards her. It slid on to the floor. She eased herself from underneath it and grabbed the end by Iain's feet. Using all her strength, she pulled the mattress across her room and squeezed it through the door. She staggered breathless along the landing to Annabel's room, Iain snoring softly behind her. Leaving the mattress just inside the door, she gathered up some of the mess into a heap behind the bed. Time was running out. She dragged the mattress over to it and rolled Iain gently onto the floor. He snuffled and her heart leapt. She stood perfectly still, wondering what she would do if he woke up. But he didn't. When he'd been quiet for a while she tip-toed around him, collecting old knickers and shirts and dresses and piling them on top of him. When he was completely covered she bundled the mattress back into her own room.

She sat on the floor, panting and shaking. She couldn't believe what she had just done. She would never have done anything like that in Frinley. She was laughing with relief and nerves. She hardly dared go out in case he was there. She had to get herself together, be normal. She got undressed and put her scruffy jeans and horse print jumper on to help Jenni with the cleaning.

Downstairs it was worse than she'd thought. The lounge stank of old lager and sick, and there were bottles everywhere. Jenni had already filled two bin bags in the hall. And Johnnie's door had been completely kicked in. It was terrible. She didn't even want to look at his room. Jenni shouted to her from the kitchen.

'You wouldn't believe that I've been doing this for hours, would you? If you want the loo you're too late. Annabel's in there.'

Shirley shook her head.

'And your coffee's cold.'

Jenni obviously wasn't in the best mood. Shirley just sat quietly at the table and picked up her mug. Jenni was on her hands and knees scraping something off the floor with a knife.

'Don't ask me what this is, but I'll kill whoever did it.'

The whole floor was covered in grey sticky patches that had bits of grass and fag ends in them. Shirley sympathised.

'It looks disgusting.'

She watched as Jenni's scraping revealed a soft pink splodge beneath the grey.

'I mean, what the hell is it?'

Shirley eyed it guiltily. It looked very much like a marsh-mallow.

'Search me.' Her voice sounded rather high. 'I'll start hoovering, shall I?' She fled to the hall.

'With that thing? You'd be better off pushing a stick round. Anyway, its bag's full. You'll have to recycle it again.'

When Annabel and her mystery man came out of the bath-room Shirley was squatting on the hall floor pulling fluff and hair out of the hoover bag. So far she'd found an earring and 57p. And something she hoped was a balloon. She smiled at them nervously as they went back upstairs. She knew they'd found him when she heard the screams.

'A pervert. Oh my God. There's a pervert in my bedroom. Get him out, get him out.'

Iain came charging down the stairs, still in his socks.

'I was asleep, honest. All night. I don't even know how I got there.'

He slammed the front door as Annabel came after him, bran-dishing a hairdryer.

'Who was that weirdo? Did you know him?'

Shirley's heart was racing but she didn't show it. She looked straight at Annabel and lied.

Chapter 13

Telling The Folks

Andy held out the phone. 'Okay, who's going first?'

Anna laughed nervously, 'You're not serious?'

'Why not? It's got to be done sometime. We might as well do it all together.'

She took the phone out of his hand and put it down. 'Why? Why does it have to be done?'

Cass shrugged. 'Don't look at me, I'm with Andy.'

'But I don't see why they have to be told.'

Andy sat next to her on the sofa. 'Listen, sweetie, I understand how you feel. I'm not wild about my folks either. And if we're talking tears and tantrums here, well, it was years ago, but believe me, you do not want to go there. But this little baby is something so wonderful in my life that I want them to know about it. After all, they're going to be grandparents.'

'Yeah, but what if they're not happy about it?'

'Ha. When are they ever happy? I don't expect them to be popping champagne corks, sweetie, I just want them to know.'

Anna sighed. 'But don't you care what they say?'

'If I cared about that I'd be living with a neutered moggy in Surbiton.' He smiled at her. 'Listen, honey, don't be fooled by this rugged exterior. I can't stand them, never see them, don't care about them. I'm still nervous as a kitten.'

'Looks like it's me first, then.' Cass had the phone in her hand. It was ringing.

'Ansaphone.' She held up the receiver. 'Listen to this, it's a classic.'

They could hear low chanting in the background and two voices speaking in rhythm. 'You have reached a machine that speaks with the voices of Sky and Jeffrey. We choose not to be controlled by the demands of the technoverse, but if you leave a message we will weave your song into the pattern of our lives.'

She grimaced at the others. 'They're so embarrassing.' The beeping stopped.

'This is Cassandra. I've got news. Anna's pregnant. You're going to be grandparents. Our friend Andy's the father. Speak to you whenever.'

She put the phone down. 'Right, that's me done. Who's next?'

Andy laughed. 'God, Cass, how to follow that?'

She shrugged. 'It's cool. They'll be fine about it.'

'Unlike mine, then.' He took the phone. 'Here goes nothing.' They counted the seconds until it was answered.

'Hello, Mum. It's Andy . . . I know, I keep meaning to phone. I know how busy you are . . . Fine, yeah. How's the family? . . . Good, that's great . . . Actually, Mum, I rang to tell you something . . . No, it's nothing terrible . . . What do you mean you knew it would come to this? You don't know what I'm going to say.' His face closed down. 'No I have not got AIDS!'

He threw the phone onto the sofa and looked at the others.

'Shall I scream at her or just cut her off and pretend I'm an orphan?'

Anna was shocked. She hushed him. 'Neither, she's only worried about you, that's all.'

He smiled with a practised patience and patted her hand. 'You don't know her like I do, sweetie. She's all for my so-called sins catching up on me.'

He looked over to Cass, who was leaning on the piano. 'What do you think?'

She shrugged. 'I'd tell her. Why not blow her mind?'

He smiled at her. 'Oh, you really are a tough cookie.' He picked up the phone.

'Listen, Mum, I'm back and I'm going to tell you my news because it's probably the best news you'll ever get from me . . . Are you ready? . . . I'm going to be a dad . . . Mum, did you hear me?'

He covered the phone. 'She's not saying anything. I think she's crying.'

Anna urged him back. 'That's good.'

'Mum, are you there? . . . I know, I couldn't believe it either, but it's true. In fact he, she or it is sitting right next to me . . . Well, her name's Anna and she's a very nice thirty-something.' Anna rolled her eyes at him. 'And Cass is here too, she's the other mummy, a not-so-nice twenty-something.' He raised his arm against the cushion flying towards him. 'That's right, two mummies . . . I know it's unconventional, but I was never going to be the married-with-2.4-kids type, was I? . . . Not my scene . . . anyway, we can't marry each other.' He looked up at Cass. 'Not that these girls wouldn't make a lovely pair of brides, bless 'em.' She sneered back. 'What? Bigamy?' He put his hand over his mouth. 'Mum, I think you've got the wrong end of the stick here, I'm not having a relationship with them. I'm still gay. Anna and Cass are lesbians, Mum. They're a couple . . . Mum, are you still there? . . . Mum?'

The phone had gone dead. 'She's hung up on me.' He ran his hands through his hair. 'I didn't handle that very well, did I?'

He smiled at them, then got up to put the phone back in the hall. He stayed there for some time. When he came back his mood had changed. Anna and Cass exchanged glances.

'For fuck's sake I've been out for twenty years. And not only that, she thought I'd got a fucking harem on the go. I mean, puh-lease. It's not just that I'm through my homo-phase and back to hetty-ville. Oh no. She really believed I was screwing around with two women at once. From bugger to bigamist in one fell swoop. No offence, girls, but it's a pretty tacky idea.'

'None taken, I agree.' Cass moved over to the sofa and sat on the arm. Anna gestured for him to join them. He sat in the middle and put his head on her shoulder.

'Well, isn't this fabulous fun?' He turned to Anna. 'I suppose now you've seen how well it's all going, you'll want to ring your parents.'

Anna looked away. 'Um ... it's not that simple. My parents ...' She hesitated, glancing across at Cass. 'Well, the thing is ...'

Andy took her hand. 'It's all right, sweetie, don't get in a state. I wasn't serious.'

But Cass was watching her. 'The thing is what?'

There was a long pause.

'They don't know.'

Cass leant forward. 'What don't they know?'

Anna was looking sheepish. 'They don't know I'm a lesbian.'

Cass frowned. 'Sorry, I'm confused here. I thought you told them when you saw them last summer. We talked about it.'

'No, we didn't. I said I didn't want to talk about it, remember? I just said it didn't go well.'

Andy shrank back into the sofa, trying to disappear.

'But I thought you meant that they didn't take it well. That's why I didn't push you on it.'

'I know you did. I let you think that.'

'But you didn't tell them?'

'No'. Anna shook her head. 'Look, I couldn't do it. I tried, but I just couldn't get the words out. I knew you'd be angry and disappointed so I just let you think that I had.'

Cass got up from the sofa.

'Let me just get this right. You're about to have a baby with me, but you haven't told your parents that you're a lesbian?'

'No.'

'And what about the child? Are you planning to tell our child that we're together?'

'Of course I am. That's not fair, Cass.'

'Yes it is.' They were both shouting.

Andy got up. 'Look, I think I'd better go out or something. This is for the two of you to sort out.'

'No, Andy, this is about all of us.' Cass gestured for him to sit down again and Anna pulled him by the jumper.

'Anna, if we're not open and positive about our family what does that say to our child? We have to be proud about who we are so that they can be too.'

'I know that.' She put her hands over her belly. 'But we don't have to tell everybody. We have to protect this baby from all the shit out there.'

'Well, you won't protect it by hiding.'

They were quiet for a while, then Cass sat in front of Anna and put her hands over hers. Her voice was softer. 'Our family is in the front line and that's a hard place to be. But we don't have a choice. The only way things are going to change is if we make them change.'

Andy put his hands over theirs. 'We'll be all right, Anna. We'll do it together.'

Anna moved them away.

'I'm sorry, but I don't want to tell the world about us. I know you two are really strong about all this, but I don't *want* to be different. I just want to be normal, like everyone else. Why should I tell people that I'm gay, or that we're a gay family and expose myself to their judgement?'

Cass shrugged and got up. 'I think I've just said why.'

'But if I tell my parents, what's the point? They're in their seventies. They're a different generation. They think I'm the original girl-next-door.'

When Cass didn't answer, Andy intervened.

'You are, honey, just the type an old dyke like Cass goes for. Isn't that right, Cass?' There was a moody silence. 'Okay, girls, if we're going to have this row again, can I at least get us a drink?' He got up to go to the kitchen. 'And no scrapping while I'm gone, I've just hoovered.'

Anna turned to Cass. 'Maybe I should call them.'

'Up to you.'

'I know you're right. I should tell them. It's just that . . .' She trailed off. 'Okay, I'll do it.' She took a deep breath. 'It's the right thing to do. Get me the phone. I want to do it.'

Cass blew her a kiss as Andy came back in.

'Ah, now that's what I like to see. Romance.'

The phone rang. They all looked at each other. He was the first to speak.

'I'll get it. It's bound to be my mother ringing me back for round two.'

He went into the hall.

'Hello . . . Yes it is . . . Sorry, who is this? Sky, oh right . . . Thanks . . . Yes, it's great, we're all ecstatic . . . end of February . . . Yes, she is, yes . . . I'll get her.'

He came in with the phone. 'It's your mum, Cass.' She took it and he turned to Anna. 'Isn't it gratifying to know that even hippies can weave 1471 into the pattern of their lives?'

'Hi, Sky. Thanks, I know . . . She's fine, doing really well . . . A party? Oh, I don't know.' Anna was shaking her head, looking horrified. Cass's parents were a little overwhelming. 'Perhaps after the baby's born? . . . We'd love to see you too . . . Yes, that'd be great . . . Listen, we'll talk about it nearer the birth, but I don't think Anna will go for it . . . Okay, love you too . . . I'll kiss her for you . . . And him . . . Bye.'

When she got off the phone, Andy gave her a glass of wine.

'Let's toast our first happy grandparent. Thank God there are some unfucked-up people out there.'

Cass laughed. 'You haven't met my parents yet, have you?'

'No, but don't spoil the moment with the horrible truth.' He clinked their glasses. 'To our strange and extraordinary family.' Anna took slow sips.

'I wish my parents were more like yours.'

'What, you mean swap their cardies for a caftan? I don't think so.'

'Why not?'

'Well, for a start, my parents want us to ritually eat the placenta. Sky's got a recipe for you.'

'Agh!' Andy was appalled. 'That's disgusting.'

'I know. Placenta pâté. I wasn't going to tell you.'

He pulled a face. 'I wish you hadn't.'

'Anna, you know my parents. They want me to be different.

The more outrageous I am the better. If I told them I was getting married and settling down they'd have a fit. What would they tell their friends? They'd be the laughing stock of the New-Age circuit. This way I'm an asset. I can hear them now, "My daughter's girlfriend is pregnant, we're so proud." It's the only way Sky would admit to being a grandmother.'

Andy refilled his glass. 'Well, pâté aside, that sounds good to me.'

'Yeah, I'm not denying that they're good like that. But I'm a trendy accessory, like I've always been. Sky joined the hippy trail to India because brown babies were in vogue. And she got what she wanted. Me. She was three months gone when she met Jeffrey, and she only got it on with him, as she puts it, because he'd meditated with George Harrison. My mother is profoundly superficial.'

Anna sighed. 'You're just exaggerating now.'

'You think so? Well, next time you see Sky, try calling her Sylvia and see what the reaction is. Or see what happens if I call her Mum. She doesn't want to be my mum. They've never wanted to, you know that. Your parents may be dull, Anna, but at least they're on the same planet. When I was a child and needed them, they were always too stoned or stressed out to deal with me. Of course it's fine now, because I'm off their hands.' She turned to Andy. 'When I was fifteen and having a hard time, Sky just dumped me at Greenham Peace Camp. I didn't even want to go. They wanted me to. It took me a long time to forgive her for that. I'm not saying they're as bad as yours or anything. But they're by no means perfect, believe me.'

She stopped. Anna had the phone in her hand.

'Hello, Dad, it's Anna. . . . Were you? I was just thinking about you too . . . How are you both? . . . Oh dear . . . She had that quite nasty before, didn't she? . . . Old Mr Punter? Has he? . . . Well, he had been ill for some time. Send my condolences to Mrs Punter . . . That's still aching, is it? . . . Arthritis, you said that, didn't you?'

She made a face at Cass, who was urging her on.

'Listen, Dad, there's something I wanted to tell you and

Mum. In fact I've wanted to say something for quite a long time, but didn't know how. It's about me and Cass . . . You know we've been living together for a long time now, well, I don't know how to say this, but we're more than just friends.' She had been staring at her knees but now she looked up. 'What do you mean you know? . . . Why didn't you say anything? . . . I thought you'd be upset. I don't know, that you wouldn't love me any more.' She was smiling. 'I know I'm silly. I really wish I'd said something . . . Yes, put her on . . . Mum, I don't believe this . . . No, I didn't think you were too old, of course not.'

She looked guiltily at the other two.

'I can't believe how well you're taking it all . . . What do you mean you've had years to get used to it? How long have you known? . . . No I'm still here . . . I was just thinking, you know, I've been so worried, thinking that you wouldn't want to know me and well, Cass and I have argued about it a lot, and all the time you were just waiting for me to tell you . . . No, it's just that I feel stupid. All these years pretending that Cass slept in the back room, and you knew . . . No, it was up to me, it's my fault . . .'

She made a face at Cass, who was pointing to her stomach.

'Mum, there's something else I've got to tell you. You might be quite shocked but it's something Cass and I have wanted for a long time. We're starting a family, Mum. We're having a baby with our friend Andy. I'm pregnant . . . It's a shock, I know . . . the end of February . . . It's probably best if you talk to Dad . . . That's right, grandparents . . . Okay, I'll let you go then . . . I know, it's as unexpected as I was all those years ago . . . In a hospital, yes . . . That's very rare now, with all the modern technology . . . Mum, I really don't want to think about that business with Auntie Dora. I'm sure they don't let students even do the stitching any more.'

Andy had his hand over his mouth in horror. Anna waved him away.

'Anyway, these days they're more likely to know what it should look like . . . yes, I'll be sure to check it all carefully afterwards, just to make sure . . . Dad's what? You'd better get him to a chair . . . Bye. I love you both. Bye.'

She put the phone down slowly. 'They knew. For years, they've known and they didn't say anything. I can't believe that they didn't say anything. They just let all that pretence carry on.'

Cass took the phone from her and gave it to Andy.

'You know why they didn't say anything. Because they were too bloody nice to mention it. You're just like them, Anna.'

She smiled. 'I suppose I am, yes.'

'Anyway,' Andy was pouring himself more wine, 'you should be happy. They still love you, you're still a nice girl and they're going to be grandparents.'

'I know, I can't get over it. Weren't they good about it all? I think they're really excited.' She kissed Cass. 'I feel so relieved. I want to kiss you both.'

When she moved towards Andy she noticed the tears in his eyes.

'Oh Andy, I'm sorry. I'm being selfish. I'm sure your mum will ring back, you know.'

He emptied his glass. 'Listen, I'm not thinking about her. These are tears of happiness, darling. This is our big day, the day we made our baby official and nobody, but nobody, is going to spoil it.'

Chapter 14

The Café in Crisis

'So Shirley doesn't know you're here then, Pearl?

'She's got no idea, Cass. I'm going to surprise her when she gets home from college. I can't wait to see her face when she sees me.' She paused over the pastries. 'To tell you the truth, I only decided myself this morning. It was one of my wild ideas. I was sorting out Gordon's golf socks and I thought stuff this, I'm off to see Shirley.' She pointed to a date slice. 'Is she really all right? You would tell me, wouldn't you?'

Cass reached across the counter with the tongs. 'She's fine, Pearl, really. You don't need to worry. Now, that's a pot of tea and a cake. £1.60 please.'

Pearl had spotted a leaflet on the display rack, 'The Fragrant Womb: Aromatherapy and the Menopause'. She picked it up and held out a £50 note. Cass opened the till.

'Have you got anything smaller?'

Pearl looked at her distractedly. 'Oh, sorry. That's not for you, dear. I'm in the wrong side of my purse. I found a few of these fifties hidden at the back of Gordon's pants drawer. I'm going to buy Shirley a new dress and a night out. His treat.'

They both smiled and Pearl gave her the right change.

'It's very quiet in here this afternoon.'

'Hmm, I know. It's the December weather. It keeps people indoors.'

Pearl nodded, eyeing the empty tables. 'Well, at least you've got one full table, so I'm not your only customer.'

Cass gave her the tray. 'Actually, you are. They all work here. To be honest, Pearl, we're having a meeting about whether to close the café down.'

'What? Because of a few quiet afternoons?'

'It's not just that. I suppose I may as well tell you. We've had the Environmental Health people here and they're not too happy with us. Basically, we've got eight weeks until they come back. Then we're finished.'

She felt quite tearful talking about it. She'd come to the café eight years before when she'd finally left Greenham. It had been her first proper job and her first proper home. The collective had let her live in one of the empty rooms upstairs for almost a year. But that was a long time ago. Cass was the only one who remembered those days now, all the others had moved on, and the people on the new collective were very different. They had no idea about how much work had gone into getting the café off the ground. In the early days they had all shared the responsibilities as well as the profits, but now the ideals had faded. People had drifted away and others had drifted in. She wondered how much they would really care if it all went down the tubes.

Pearl was looking around. 'I don't see why you should close. This place has got bags of potential.' She chewed on the date slice. 'You'd be amazed what you can do in eight weeks. I could work wonders in that time. You should have seen me with my kitchen last summer. I had these terrible units. Years old. Brown and orange formica, well, you can imagine, can't you? I couldn't let anyone in there for shame. Anyway, Gordon, typical man, only went and invited the entire golf club to his fiftieth. I told him straight, I said "Gordon, over my dead body. Graham Gillingham's wife is not setting foot in this house until you do something about the state of my surfaces." Of course, he just ignored me like normal. But I snapped. I was like a mad thing.

I gutted that kitchen with my own bare hands. Two weeks we lived like that. Chaos. Shirley hated me. Gordon wasn't speaking. We'd got no units, not even a sink, and he wouldn't say a word about it. Anyway, even he can't wash up in a bucket for ever, so eventually he came round. Bought me a new kitchen, country oak and pastel yellow. I love it.'

Cass smiled. 'Anyway, I'd better get back to the meeting. If you want anything else, just give me a shout.'

Pearl nodded and pointed to the leaflet. 'I'll be fine with this.' Cass left her reading about the menopausal marvels of marjoram.

She joined the others. 'Okay, so you've all read the Environmental Health report. The question is, what do we do about it?'

Mel interrupted. 'No, the question is what do we *want* to do about it?' She was sitting on a stool behind Dave, plaiting his pony-tail. Her legs were wrapped around his waist, and his head was nestled in the folds of her batik dungarees. He was blowing bubble-gum bubbles and stroking the hair around her ankles.

Cass stared at her. 'What's that supposed to mean?'

'You're the one with all the answers, Cass, what do you think it means?'

Dave smirked. Mel pulled his head back and kissed him, sucking the gum out of his mouth. She came up chewing.

Dave hadn't been working at the café for long, and if Cass had stood her ground he wouldn't have been there at all. It was another reason that she and Mel didn't get on. Mel had brought him to the meetings and put him forward to be a member of the collective, but Cass had argued against him. His week's trial had shown that he was as useless on the counter as he was in the kitchen. What Cass didn't know then, but was soon to find out, was that what he lacked in catering talent he made up for in the bedroom. Mel's bedroom. And she wasn't going to let him slip through her fingers. The grief involved in blocking him simply hadn't been worth it and Cass had reluctantly voted him in.

Cass looked to the other three for support. 'Does anyone have any suggestions about how we can deal with this?'

Jasbinder was sitting precariously on the stool next to Mel.

She had pulled her legs right up to her chin and was hugging her shins. This was always her reaction to tension in the collective. Whenever meetings got heated she tried to disappear. Cass caught her eye and Jaz whispered something non-committal to her kneecap. It was hard to believe that Jaz had a prison record for criminal damage. She'd grafittied and smashed windows at three universities involved in animal experiments, and Cass knew from other people that she'd been involved in break-ins at an Oxfordshire fur farm. She was surprisingly strong too. At just seven stone and five foot nothing, she could carry a sack of soya up to the kitchen more easily than any of them.

At the end of the table Dee was sitting back in her chair, ignoring them all. She was holding the report over her face, reading it slowly. Dee was Cass's favourite person at the café. She was a big Jamaican woman with a peculiar air of detachment and a sense of humour that was often mistaken for sourness. She disliked all their customers and could be so outrageous with them that the collective had decided it was best if she worked mainly in the kitchen.

Buzz was sitting next to Cass and sneering at Mel. His jaw was twitching, which was always a bad sign. It gave him a slightly deranged look that wasn't helped by the fact that one of his eyes roamed aimlessly around the room. He'd been injured at an Anti-Nazi demo five years before when a flying brick hit him on the head. It was quite serious at the time and he'd been in hospital for several weeks. His eye was permanently damaged. It was then that he decided to give up violent struggle and work for the revolution in other ways.

Throughout the meeting, Buzz had been drumming on the table; now he stopped and spoke directly to Mel.

'I know what it means. It means you don't give a shit.'

'Fuck off, Buzz. You don't know what I think. If anyone gives a shit, it's me. But come on, people, face facts! We've got no money. We're fucked! The café's fucked! There's no point in having meetings about it. That won't change things. You've got to move on. Get a life.'

Buzz snarled at her. 'I've got a life.'

'Yeah, well it won't be here for much longer. You people should be like me and Dave. We're out of here, right, babe?' Dave mumbled something unintelligible. 'We're on tour with the Ecstastic Eggplants. Dave's brother asked me to do backing vocals. This time next week we'll be in Amsterdam. It's going to be awesome.'

Dee suddenly slapped the report down and pushed it to the middle of the table. 'Right, we'll all go to Amsterdam. Leave this mess behind and set ourselves up as the Cosmic Groupies.' She leaned back on her chair without smiling. They all looked at her. Dee rarely talked in meetings and when she did it was impossible to know how to take her. That would probably be her only contribution to the problem of how to save the café. Cass decided to ignore her.

'Okay, if no one's got any suggestions, then here's mine. I've been through the accounts and through the report and I think we can make it. There is some money, but not much. We've got just under £2,000 and we're going to need nearer ten.'

Dave scoffed. 'How much?'

'Look, Dave, there's new fridges, a new kitchen floor, all that tiling, a new counter. Even second-hand that's going to cost. Then there's the plumbing, redecorating, refitting the loos, it just goes on and on. We need money and lots of it. The bank's blown us out already, so as far as I can see there's only one solution. We'll have to raise the money ourselves.' Mel laughed mockingly but Cass took no notice. 'I've talked to Anna and she's got £3,000 I can put in. We need another five between us.'

Buzz emptied his pockets on to the table. Some rolling tobacco, papers and 78p. He looked at her with his good eye. 'Not a fucking chance, Cass.'

'Then we've got no choice, we'll have to find someone with money to join the co-op. It's the only way to get out of this mess and keep the café going. What do you think?'

Mel pointed to the counter. 'What I think is that you should serve your customer.' Cass frowned at her and she shrugged. 'It's your shift, Cass. You don't own the place yet.'

Buzz offered to go, but Cass refused. 'It's okay. I've said what

I wanted to say. I'll leave you all to think about it.' She went towards the counter. Someone was scrutinising the noticeboard.

'Hi, can I get you something?'

He turned around. It was Tony. Cass's smiled faded.

'What do you want?'

'A cup of tea please, Cass.'

She looked at him for a while before reaching for the cups.

'You've guessed I'm not here just for tea.'

She put the pot on the tray and pushed it towards him.

'To be honest, Tony, I don't care why you're here. That's 80p.'

He gave her a £5 note. 'I know you don't like me, Cass. But I want you to know that I've changed.'

She slammed the till shut. 'Right, thanks for letting me know. You can go now.'

'Look, it isn't easy for me to come here, you know, after everything that's happened. A year ago I wouldn't have come near this fucking café. But I'm different now. I want to start again with people, put the past behind me. Will you look at me, please?'

Cass had wandered to the sink. Now she came back to the counter. 'Listen, Tony, I've already put my past behind me, and you're in it. I'm glad you're a changed man now and everything, but if you've said what you've got to say I'm rather busy here.' She gestured to the collective and noticed Pearl, who was clearly eavesdropping.

'Oh, come on, Cass, don't make this even harder for me. So we're not going to be friends. Okay. I don't like you much either. We're still a part of each other's lives.'

Cass narrowed her eyes. 'Oh yeah? How do you work that one out?'

'Because me and Andy are serious.'

'And Andy put you up to this, did he?'

'No, he doesn't even know I'm here.'

'So you're going behind his back, then?'

'No. It's for him I'm doing this.'

'Doing what exactly?'

'Telling you how we feel about each other. Did you know he wants me to move in?' He watched Cass's expression change. 'I thought not. You see, he wouldn't tell you because he's worried about what you'll do.'

'Me? What's he worried about me for? I wasn't the one who cheated on him. I didn't deceive him and fuck other blokes and put him at risk of God knows what.'

'You know that's not what I meant. Listen, Cass, I know I fucked up, okay. You don't need to tell me. And I'm very sorry that I did. But I'm telling you, it's different now. Me and Andy want to be together.'

'So you said.'

'But he's scared that it'll change things with you two and the baby if I'm living at the flat.'

Cass said nothing.

'He wants to be a dad, Cass. If you make him choose between us, you'll win.'

'For God's sake, Tony. This isn't some fucking power game.'

'I'm not saying it is, I'm just telling you what's going on in Andy's head.'

'Yeah, well thanks, but I don't need you for that.'

'I think you do, Cass. Because he's not going to talk to you about this. He wants to keep me and you apart. To pretend to you that everything is fine, and there's no problem. That's why I turned up the other night.'

She stared at him. 'So you're telling me that Andy wants you to move back in with him?'

'Yes. It's what we both want.'

Tony pushed his tea back across the counter and picked up his change. Cass poured it slowly away. She watched it trickle down the drain before she spoke again.

'Last Christmas when you pissed off to Italy, Andy was gutted. He loved you and you really fucked him up. You can't just come back here, announce that you've changed, and expect everyone to love you. If Andy wants to sleep with you that's up to him. If he wants you in the flat, fine. But when our baby's born, I don't want you messing up my family.'

'I'm not going to, Cass. I love Andy, I know that now. You see, when I was in Italy something happened to me.'

'Oh yeah? What was his name?'

He ignored her gibe. 'Her name was Maria and she was my youngest sister. She was killed in January.'

Cass didn't know what to say. 'Look, I'm sorry. I didn't know.'

'I know you didn't. There're lots of things you don't know about me, that's why I want us to talk.'

He walked to the nearest table and waited for Cass to join him. He didn't look at her. When she came over, he began his story.

'In Italy I've always been the child they wanted to forget, the one they wished had never been born. When I used to visit my sisters, my parents would never see me.' He paused to light a cigarette. 'When Maria died it was different, suddenly I was their son again. I sat with my mamma and we cried together. And she hugged me like I was her lost baby, which I suppose I was, in a way. You can guess what that meant to me, after all these years.'

Cass nodded. If it had been anyone else, she would have reached out to them.

'And do you know what I realised?'

He stared at the smoke.

'I realised that for years I'd been living in defiance of them, my parents, the whole family. Proving that I didn't need anyone to love me. I was sixteen when they threw me out, eighteen when I came here. And I wanted a good time. I took risks. For years I didn't care about anyone. But when Maria died, I didn't want mamma to hold me, I wanted Andy. And I knew that I had to come back for him.'

He looked directly at her.

'I'm telling you this because I don't want to lose him again. I'll fight for him if I have to. I know he wants to be a father and I accept what's happening between the three of you. But now you have to accept me.' He stubbed out his cigarette. 'Put simply, Cass, I will not mess with your life, if you don't mess with mine.'

Cass looked over to the others. Dave and Buzz were still wrangling over how much money they'd need to save the café. Buzz was ranting about Environmental Health reports being instruments of oppression in the capitalist state. He thought they needed £8,000, Dave said three, so at least Buzz had some clue about costs. And if he was right, then maybe they had a chance. When she'd first seen the report she thought that was it – the end. The café was closing. But now she felt more hopeful. They would have to change, but perhaps that was no bad thing.

Tony stood up. She didn't like him, and given the choice, she wouldn't want him in her life. But she had no choice. If he was living with Andy then he'd be part of her life and that was that. It seemed that everything was going to be different. First the café and now this. She had to accept it, and she had to make it work.

For now.

Chapter 15

The Works Do

The restaurant was packed. Stuffed full. Anna hovered in the doorway and looked around. It was discount night for small businesses and every table sported a little red flag with the Friends in Business logo, FiB. Middle-aged men were leaning back in raffia chairs, loosening their ties and undoing trouser buttons. Women crowded around the dessert trolley, calculating calories. Andy came up behind her.

'Oh my God, pinch me! I'm having a nightmare.'

Anna smiled. 'Sorry, darling. You're still awake. This is it.'

'You mean I haven't died and gone to hell?'

'Not yet.'

'My mistake. They must have used the same decorators.'

All around them were vast murals of Roman gods frolicking behind a drapery of plastic grapes and hanging bottles of Chianti.

'I know. It's disgusting. We always come here. Mrs Granger's got something going with Luigi, the guy who owns it.'

Andy turned pale.

'You mean this is Luigi's Place?'

'Yeah. The food's good though, proper Italian.'

Andy didn't answer. He was looking around.

'Is that all right, Andy?'

He hesitated.

'Andy? Are you okay?'

'I'm fine.' He smiled at her. 'It all sounds fabulous. You know I can never say no to an Italian.'

Anna squeezed his hand. 'Come on, then. They've seen us.'

Andy braced himself. 'Hettyville here we come!'

A middle-aged woman was beckoning them from a raised table in the far corner. Anna waved back, speaking through gritted teeth.

'Smile, that's Felicity Granger.'

They pushed through the crowd.

'Anna, I'm so pleased you both finally made it. As you can see, we're all here already.'

She took the hint. 'Sorry we're late, we got held up on the train.' They'd been in the pub. Dutch courage.

'Not at all. Travis has been keeping the troops entertained with stories of his travels in Indo-China, hasn't he, everybody?' There was a rumble of assent from around the table. Travis winked at Anna. She pushed Andy forward.

'I'd like you all to meet my boyfriend, Andy.'

Mrs Granger shook him vigorously by the hand.

'So glad that you could join us, but now that you're both here, let's not waste any more time. If I can just confirm seating: Andrew, you're next to Betty and Anna's beside you.'

They both sat down where they were told. There was an empty seat next to Anna, between her and Jeannine. They smiled across it. Mrs Granger, still standing, followed Anna's gaze.

'Now, Jeannine, am I right in thinking that you've given up on anyone coming to fill that chair now?'

Jeannine coughed. 'Yes, I think so.'

'I see. Well, it would have been easier if I had known the correct numbers when I booked, but not to worry about it now. I'll have someone take it away.'

She turned back to Andy.

'Now, Andrew, as you're the new member of the group, let

me introduce you to our happy band. Although I'm sure Anna's told you all about us.'

'Believe me, Felicity, she did not do you justice.'

She laughed girlishly and Andy smiled. Anna kicked him under the table.

'Now, you're next to Betty, who has been dying to meet you, haven't you, Betty?'

Betty leant towards him in a breathy haze of sherry and lily-of-the-valley. 'I'm going to have you all to myself tonight.'

Andy bared his teeth in an uneasy smile. 'How frightening!'

She pushed him away. 'Oh, Anna. You didn't tell me he was a funny one.'

'Didn't I?' Anna smiled nervously.

'Didn't you, darling?' Andy tutted loudly. 'Believe me, Betty, I'm definitely a funny one.'

Felicity spoke over them. 'And between Betty and me is Betty's husband Larry.'

Andy held out his hand in what he considered to be a gesture of manly greeting. There was no response. Larry was slumped forward with his head just above the tablecloth, giving the uncomfortable impression of having died minutes before. Andy's hand hovered awkwardly in mid-air. Betty grasped it between her own.

'I'd leave Larry for now, Andrew, dear. He's a little shy in a crowd. Always takes his time to get going. You wait, though, he'll warm up nicely later.'

Andy nodded and turned back to Anna. 'That'll be in the crematorium, sweetie.'

'On my right here is Travis who, sadly, will be leaving us next spring on another spectacular voyage. We're all incredibly jealous.' She looked around. 'Aren't we, everyone?' They all nodded and Felicity gestured to the next chair.

'And this young lady is one of Travis's new friends, Angela. Angela is in the fascinating world of show business.'

The woman next to Travis had straight black hair and a curled red lip.

'It's Angel. And I'm training to be a performance arts therapist.' She said this with utter disdain for all of them. Andy liked her immediately.

'Moving on, we have Trevor and his wife Veronica.' Weak smiles.

'And next to them Jeannine, who, unfortunately, although booking two seats, has had to come alone.' She raised her voice. 'Waiter, could somebody do something with this chair, please?'

One of the waiters came over, followed by an older man Andy guessed to be Luigi. He looked anxiously through the swinging kitchen doors.

'Felicity.' Luigi drew out the sounds with an exaggerated Mediterranean drawl. 'So wonderful to see you here with your lovely employees.'

'Luigi.' There was a flurry of kissing.

He nodded around the table. 'This lady is the best in the business. The best FIBBER of us all.'

Felicity wagged her finger at him. 'Flatterer.'

He shrugged. 'How can I help it when I'm with such a lady as you? I just ask is it right that you should hide such beauty in a book?'

She smiled. 'You know the saying, Luigi, man cannot live by bread alone.'

'Ahhh.' He held out his arms, gesturing towards the busy tables. 'But as every businessman knows, man cannot live without it. Ha, ha.'

His laugh began as a grunt in his throat and snorted through one nostril at a time. Felicity's answering giggle was echoed by a polite titter, which edged around the table.

'And now, I will get for you my best waiter.'

He lifted his hand in the air and clicked his fingers.

'Antonio.'

As the kitchen doors swung open, Andy buried his head into the menu. He could guess what was coming. Anna's eyes widened with horror.

'Tony! Oh my God, it's Tony! I don't believe it! Tony works here!' She turned on Andy. 'Did you know that?'

He cringed helplessly into the wine list. 'Only when you said this was Luigi's. I've never been here before.'

'He's our waiter.' She looked at him wildly for a moment, then panicked and called across the restaurant.

'Hi, Tony. It's me, Anna. Just to let you know, I'm here with my boss.' Tony looked slightly bemused, but Anna was on a roll. 'Yes, I'm introducing everyone to my fiancé. You haven't met my fiancé, have you?'

She gestured to where Andy was hiding behind the menu. He was shaking his head and wouldn't let go. Tony was frowning in confusion but before he could speak, Felicity Granger started banging the table with a spoon. She pointed it at Anna.

'Did I hear the word fiancé?'

Anna blushed.

'You're getting married? Thank God for that! She gave us a scare, didn't she, Betty? We thought you'd joined the heathens!'

Betty got up and lunged towards her, arms outstretched.

'Anna, my dear, congratulations! I'm so happy for you.'

Anna stood up and they hugged awkwardly, trying to avoid the candles. Betty whispered loudly in her ear.

'There's no need to thank me, I don't expect a gift. I'm just so glad that I could help bring you two young people together, if only for the sake of the baby.'

Felicity was on her feet. 'Everybody, please fill your glasses.'

Trav reached for the wine and started pouring. Anna hissed at Andy, who still hadn't come out from behind the menu. He hissed back.

'I can't do it. I want to go home.'

She ignored him and snatched the menu away. He let out a little scream. They were all watching him. He smiled sheepishly and waggled his fingers. 'Paper cut.'

Felicity banged the table. 'Please be upstanding.' There was a shuffling of chairs as they all got up.

'A toast. To Andrew and Anna, wishing them a short engagement,' she glanced at Anna's belly, 'especially considering the circumstances, and a long and happy marriage.'

She gulped back her Chianti and to Anna's horror the whole

restaurant started to applaud. Andy grabbed the nearest bottle and poured himself another. Looking straight at Tony, he lifted his glass. 'To wedded bliss and all who sail in her.' He winked and Tony smiled back. The other tables went back to their food.

Felicity cleared her throat. She hadn't finished.

'If I may continue for a moment, Andrew? I'd just like to say a few words to you both about the great institution of marriage. Anna and Andrew, although you haven't done things in quite the proper order, I'm glad to see that you've finally made the right decision. The traditional values of marriage and family are at the heart of this society and we should do everything in our power to uphold them against those who seek to mock and condemn. It may be politically correct these days to say that any old hodgepodge shacked up in a van is a family. But I say no. A proper family has at its heart a mother and a father who are married to each other. Without that you haven't got a family, you've got a sham.

'So it makes me very happy tonight to think that when this little baby is born it will have a real family, a mummy *and* a daddy. Well done both. I now invite you all to join me in drinking to Anna and Andrew, their future together, and the preservation of decency and standards in family life.'

'Hear, hear!' Betty leant towards Andy. 'She's a born speech-maker, brings the house down at CoLiC. That's our little club you know, Conservative Ladies in Croyden.' She put down her glass and started to clap, nudging Andy to do the same. He ignored her. There was a trickle of applause as the others sat back in their seats. Only Angel was still standing, staring straight at Mrs Granger. Felicity smiled at her benevolently and gestured for her to speak.

'I'd like to add one word that I think needs saying.'

'Yes, dear?'

'Crap.'

There was stunned silence. Veronica coughed her ice back into her bitter lemon. Angel raised her glass.

'Here's to the hodgepodge and thank God for them!'

Andy was back on his feet. 'Hear, hear.' He turned to Anna, who was staring at the tablecloth.

'Anna?'

All eyes were on her. She could feel Felicity Granger's anger and disapproval. She knew that this would probably cost her her job.

'Oh, what the fuck!' She got up. 'Here's to shacking up in a van!'

Andy smiled. He clinked her glass. 'And here's to speaking out! Well done, sweetie.'

On the other side of the table, Trav started to laugh. 'What's this? Little Anna being radical? That's a new one.'

Anna flushed and narrowed her eyes at him. 'Oh, I can do better than that.' She raised her glass again and looked around the table. 'Here's to speaking out and coming out!'

Andy squeezed her hand. 'Brave girl.'

Trav grinned. 'Coming out? I never saw you as a little debutante, Anna. Or are you just coming out of your shell?'

He leant back in his chair, smirking.

'I'm not a snail, Trav, I'm a lesbian. I'm coming out of the closet.'

Chapter 16

Pearl's Night Out

The taxi ambled around the corner of Madrigal Road with Shirley directing from the back.

'Yes, that's it. Just a bit further, a bit more, nearly there, a little bit more, that's it, just another little bit. Oh, you've stopped.'

The driver grunted and flicked the ceiling light. He held out his hand.

'£12.80.'

'Oh right, yes, the money. I'll just get it.'

She nudged her mum, who was slumped next to her. There was no response. The driver turned back around and began a bored and breathy whistling.

'Mum, wake up!'

Shirley pulled Pearl's handbag out from where she was sitting on it and started rummaging for her purse. Her mum slid across the seat and flopped against the door. Shirley held out the last £50 note.

'I can't find anything smaller. Is this okay?'

He mumbled something humourless about a tip and snatched it from her hand. Suddenly the car lurched forward. Pearl streaked across the windowpane, leaving a smear of bright fuschia LushLips in her wake. Shirley could hear laughing behind them as their driver jumped out. She looked out of the back window and saw another taxi.

'Gary, you wanker!'

'Gotcha, Stan, you old fucker! That's another ten points for me.'

'You slimy bleeder, I'm gonna 'ave you! I'm gonna shaft your arse off!'

'Whoa! Big talk, bumper bender!'

Shirley stopped listening. Her mum was still squashed against the window. She gave her a shake.

'Come on, Mum, we're home.'

Pearl moaned and her head rolled backwards with a jolt. She looked around woozily. 'Where are we?'

'Home.'

'Where's Gordy?'

'Dad's not here. You left him in Frinley.'

Pearl grunted meaningfully. 'If only!' She slumped back against the seat.

Shirley got out of the taxi. Their driver had the other one in a headlock and was pretending to whack him against the bonnet. Shirley edged around them and thought glumly about their £50. Her mum would have to get it. She opened the other door and Pearl flopped out on to the road.

'Ow!'

Shirley heaved her up. She staggered under her mum's weight and they swayed across the pavement. When they were steady, Shirley explained their financial predicament. Her lament about the £50 note had a brief but powerfully sobering effect on her mother. Pearl raised her head.

'You gave him what? Shirley, what have I told you about taxi drivers and large notes?'

Shirley replied with bewildered honesty. 'Nothing.'

'Ooh.' Her mother rolled her eyes as if this was the umpteenth time they'd been through this, and teetered over to where the drivers were still scuffling. She stood with her hands on her hips, an imposing sight made more frightening by the garish smudge across her left cheek.

'Which one of you has got my fifty?'

They both looked up. Stan held up a scrunch of paper still clasped in his hand.

While her mother sorted out the change down to the last penny and no tip, Shirley watched the scene in the other car. Anna from across the road was sitting on the backseat with her head in her hands while a man who looked like their estate agent tried to get her out of the cab. If her mum saw them, she was bound to make a scene.

As soon as Pearl had shut her purse, Shirley grabbed her by the arm and escorted her up their path. Her mother was complaining loudly about the price of the fare.

'Just because I've had a few pink gins, he thinks he can take me for a mug. £12.80 indeed! They see you coming, Shirley, they really do! We'd only gone the length of our road at home.'

'It's London, Mum. It's what it costs.'

'London, my arse. He's ripping us off! I said to him, What's this? A travelling circus! I'm not paying you to act like a fat Hulk Hogan. You can have five quid, and think yourself lucky I'm not ringing your employer.'

'Right, Mum, that's it.' Shirley got out her key. 'When we get inside we're going straight upstairs.'

'Why? Aren't we going to say hello to everyone?'

'No.'

'Oh dear! Shirley, I feel bad.'

'What now?'

'I feel sick.'

'No, Mum, please don't. Not there! . . . Oh no!'

Shirley watched horrified as her mum crouched down and vomited all over the privet. 'I don't believe this! How could you!'

'I'm so sorry, Shirley. I feel terrible.'

'Wait there!'

Shirley left Pearl on the pavement and ran inside for a bucket of water. It took two buckets full to sloosh down the hedge, so it was a while before Shirley noticed that her mum had gone. She ran out into the street looking for her, calling her in a loud and irritated whisper. When there was no response she ran back inside and up to her room. It was empty. Then she tried the kitchen, the bathroom and the lounge. Nothing. She was beginning to panic when she heard noises coming from Johnnie's room. Her stomach clenched. Praying that it wasn't who she thought it was, she pressed her ear to the door to make sure. Her mother's voice rang out clearly through the plyboard. 'Who'd have thought I'd be smoking pot at my age?'

Shirley winced. 'Shit! Shit! Shit!' She debated the least embarrassing course of action. She could go in there and haul her mum out before she made a total fool of herself, which risked a scene in front of Johnnie and Ruby; or she could just go to bed and hope that Pearl would fall asleep within the next five minutes. She paused for barely a second before tip-toeing up the stairs.

On the other side of the door Pearl was taking a tentative drag on the joint and slouching back into Johnnie's armchair.

'Are you sure you don't mind me barging in on you like this?'

Johnnie and Ruby were stoned and giggling together under the blankets.

'It's just that Shirley – and I'm only saying this because I'm her mother – well, she can be a bit boring. She gets that from her father. You know what men can be like. I mean, fancy going to bed at ten! That's just like him.' She took another puff. 'I know you two are in bed, but that's different.'

Johnnie was trying to pull his shorts on under the covers. Ruby wasn't helping. Pearl coughed.

'If there's any chance of a coffee, I'll have three sugars in mine.'

Their heads appeared above the sheets and Ruby pushed Johnnie on to the floor.

'I think that's your job, *darling*, unless, of course, you want to stay here and chat with Shirley's mother?'

Johnnie pouted at her. 'No thanks, *darling*! I'll make the

drinks.' He stuffed his hands under the sheets, making Ruby scream at him before leaving them to it. Pearl watched him go.

'Hasn't he got a lovely body? You know that's what I need. Some bloody good sex!'

Ruby sat up, flattening her hair. 'It works for me.'

Pearl grunted. 'It seems to work for Shirley's father too. You won't believe this, but last night I found out that Gordon, that old stuffed shirt I'm married to, is having an affair with my best friend.' She sniffed and wiped her nose on the sleeve of her silk blouse. 'I mean, how could she do it to me?'

Ruby wrapped herself in the sheet and squatted by Pearl's chair. She lit another joint. 'Smoke this. Believe me, it helps.'

Pearl took it and smiled. 'You'll never guess how I found out. We were all at Gordon's golf club playing that terrible game, Marital Pursuits. Have you played it?'

Ruby shook her head.

'Well, you're not missing much.'

Pearl took a drag on the joint and coughed loudly. 'My head's gone all funny.' She passed it to back Ruby.

'That's good, you're getting stoned.'

'So there we were, me and Gordon, Keith and Pam Smedley, and Barbara and Barry Barlow, who I've never liked. Then Pam landed on the Getting Your Nuptials square, which meant all the women had to answer the question: what's the worst thing you've ever had in your mouth?

'Of course Barbara, who was the worse for wear by this point, was immediately in with Barry's penis, which made me feel sick after what she'd told me about his eczema. Then it was me. So I said, no doubt about it, it was a bad pickled egg I'd had in Morecambe Bay in 1967. So then we were waiting for Pam. Oh, she says as if butter wouldn't melt, I think it has to be a golf sock. That was when it hit me. I could see Gordon sniggering into his martini, and I thought, you wanker. You've been having it off with Pam Smedley. They're golf partners, you see, ever since Keith got his frozen shoulder.'

She took back the joint for another drag.

'I didn't say anything at the time, but this morning I went

straight to his golf bag and I found it. The evidence. The toes of his golf socks were smeared with lipstick. And as soon as I saw that pink, I knew. It was Loud Raspberry. And it could only be Pam because she bulk-bought when Avon stopped doing it.'

Another drag.

'You've never smelt one of Gordon's golf socks, have you? Take my word for it, if she's putting that in her mouth, they've been playing more than eighteen holes.'

Ruby was smiling, thinking about Shirley and the hairy toe-sucker. She was more like her father than she realised.

'That's what she does for him, you see. He's asked me for it, but I told him. I said the only place I'm stuffing your socks, Gordon, is in the bleeding washing machine. I mean it's not hygienic. It's not as if I'm a prude, don't get me wrong. I'm not bothered if he sticks his foot where I can't taste it. But if Pam Smedley is putting that sock in her mouth then they are well beyond sex and into the truly perverse. It's an obsession with him. All he wants to do is stick his sock into something rude.'

Johnnie kicked the door open to bring in the coffees and his slippered foot poked around the doorframe. Pearl and Ruby looked at each other and collapsed with giggles. They waggled their toes and spluttered into their coffees. Johnnie smiled at them and rolled himself a joint.

'You know, I don't really blame Gordon for this. In fact, for the first time in years, I think he's got the right idea. Why should we just sit it out in a miserable marriage? It's not as if Shirley's at home now.'

Pearl flopped back in the chair.

'Why should I sit in bloody Frinley day in day out until they carry me out in a box? It's not as if I haven't got savings, I've always tucked away a bit of the housekeeping. It adds up over twenty-odd years, you know. I could go anywhere.'

She closed her eyes and let her head roll back. She was quiet for so long they thought she'd gone to sleep. But she'd been thinking.

'I'd say there's hope for me yet.'

Chapter 17

Back To Work

It was late Saturday morning when Ruby pushed open Anna's bedroom door. 'Hope you're decent. I've made us some tea.'

Anna was still under the duvet. 'Go away!'

'Charming!'

'I know why you're here and I'm not going!'

'I don't know what you mean.'

'Don't lie! Cass sent you, didn't she?'

'Cass who?'

'Ha, ha.'

'All right, yes. She rang me from the café.'

'So I suppose you know about what happened last night.'

'Yes, and I'm very proud of you.'

Anna just moaned and turned over.

'Now what's wrong?'

'You don't understand. It's all a disaster. I can't believe I did it.'

Ruby flung open the curtains. 'I can! And I think it's the best thing you've done in years. About time you stood up to that cow.'

'That's what Cass said, but that cow happens to be my boss.

Correction, was my boss.' Anna propped herself up and sipped at the tea.

Ruby was shocked. 'She didn't sack you?'

'No, but only because we left. Anyway, it doesn't matter now because I can never go back.'

'Why not?'

Anna looked at her as if she was stupid. 'Because of what I said last night.'

'What did you say that was so terrible?'

Anna grunted at her and went back under the duvet.

'You can't just give up your job because they know you're a dyke.'

There was a muffled 'Why not?' from under the duvet.

'Because that means you lose out and they all carry on being bastards.'

'I can live with that.'

'But why should you?'

No answer.

'How long have you been working there?'

'Eight years.'

Ruby was exasperated. 'Right, I'm going to ring that bookshop and give them a piece of my mind.' Anna looked up, but Ruby was in full swing. 'No, I've got a better idea.' She was heading down the stairs. 'I'm going there in person to ball that woman out.'

Anna jumped out of bed. 'Ruby, no! You can't.'

'Just watch me.'

Anna ran to the banister and called down. 'She's not there on Saturday.'

'I don't believe you!' The front door slammed.

Anna dashed back to the bedroom window. She could see Ruby striding down the Close. She banged on the glass. 'Stop!' Ruby looked up. Anna opened the window.

'You can't do this to me. I'll never live it down.'

Ruby shouted back. 'But it won't matter. You're not going back there, remember?'

Anna screwed her face up at her. 'Well, perhaps I might. On Monday maybe, or Tuesday.'

Ruby walked back. 'Anna, if you don't go in for your shift today, she'll use it as an excuse to fire you.' She paused for her to think about it. When there was no response, she spelt it out. 'It's now or never, girl. I'll give you five minutes.'

Anna sat back on the bed and closed her eyes. By the time Ruby came back for her, she was dressed.

When they got to the shop it was busy. There was only one more Saturday before Christmas and the festive buying frenzy was in full swing. Both Trev and Trav were serving. Anna hovered by the door until Ruby pushed her though it. Trevor was the first to notice them. He blushed wildly and in one swift movement locked his eyes to the floor and his hands to his groin. Ruby clocked him.

'What's he holding his dick for?'

'Ruby, shush.'

'Well, what does he think you're going to do, make a grab for it?'

Anna pushed her through hobbies and towards the back stairs. 'It's fine. I don't want to speak to any of them anyway.'

It was too late. Trav had seen her. He shouted to her from the till. She turned around and he gave her a clenched fist salute.

'Yo sister!'

Anna flushed and turned away. Trav laughed.

'Oh come on, Anna, I was joking.' He came out from behind the till and pointed at Ruby. 'Is this your girlfriend?'

Ruby answered before Anna had a chance. 'I'm Ruby.'

'Hi! Les-be-friends.'

She sneered at him.

'Hey, it was a joke!'

Trav reached over to Anna with his arms out. 'Let me show you my support.' He held her in an uneasy hug, then drew away. 'Well, Anna, you really had me fooled. You're a proper little actress, aren't you?' Anna was flustered. She started to mumble denial. Trav rammed himself against her, kissing her wetly on the mouth. Ruby pulled him off.

'Hey, call off your girlfriend! I was just being friendly, or can't a man even touch you now? I mean I'm on your side. Sisters doing it for themselves and all that.'

Ruby stood between them. 'Too right when you're the alternative.' She looked him up and down.

Anna turned tail and ran down the stairs.

Felicity Granger was standing in her office doorway watching the handful of familiar customers browsing in the basement. When she saw Anna her gaze hardened. 'You've got a nerve to show your face here.'

Anna was silent. She had lost all the bravado of the night before. She didn't want a scene. She turned to go but Ruby was in her way. Anna pushed past her.

'Leave it, Ruby, I'm going home.'

Ruby grabbed her hand. 'Not yet you're not. Not like this.' She shouted across to Felicity Granger, who was now sitting in her office with the door shut. 'Anna's here because she works here.' There was no response.

'If you've dismissed her, I would like to know why. Just for the record.'

Felicity came to the door. 'If you do not both leave the shop at once I will have you escorted out.'

But Ruby was undeterred.

'Do I take it then that Anna is dismissed?'

Felicity narrowed her eyes but refused to speak. Ruby wouldn't let it go.

'On what grounds is she sacked?'

Felicity snapped. 'On any grounds I like. Now get out.'

'You are aware that she is seven months pregnant?'

'I'm aware that she's a pervert.'

Ruby was in control. 'And are you also aware that there are laws against such discrimination?'

'What? Who the hell do you think you are?'

Ruby smiled. 'Did I not introduce myself? How clumsy of me. My name's Ruby Kavanagh, I'm Anna's lawyer, employment law is my specialism. Anna asked me to come along with her to this meeting. Quite wisely, it seems now.'

Felicity Granger blanched.

'I'll just need the names of the witnesses and it looks like we'll be seeing you at a tribunal. How does unfair dismissal sound?' Ruby turned to Anna, who was sitting on the stairs with her head in her hands. 'We've got her worried now.'

Anna groaned. The last thing she needed was to sit there and listen to Ruby's play-acting. She turned around and ran back up the stairs, through the shop and out on to the street.

It was ten minutes before Ruby came out to find her. She strode over. 'What a fantastic way to get men's phone numbers. Call them witnesses and they just hand them right over. Look!' She held up several scraps of paper. 'I'm going to ring that one. He was gorgeous!'

Anna sighed and started walking.

Ruby stuffed the numbers in her bag and caught up. 'Anyway, what did you think? "Ruby Kavanagh Fighting for Justice".'

Anna didn't stop. 'Ruby, I know you're trying to help and everything, but I just wanted to get out of there. Nothing you say will do any good. There is no law against gay discrimination.'

Ruby exaggerated surprise. 'Isn't there? Are you sure? Well, don't tell the Gorgon Granger that.'

Anna snapped. 'I don't need to tell her, do I? She's already sacked me!' She turned away, mumbling bitterly to herself. 'I knew I shouldn't have come. It was a complete waste of time.'

'I wouldn't quite say that.'

Anna looked round. 'Why? What have you done?'

'I merely pointed out the extortionate cost of legal representation if it came to a tribunal.' Ruby smiled at her. 'And I might have mentioned, off the record, that when your friends in Outrage! got to hear about it, the demonstrations would be very embarrassing.'

'But I don't know anyone in Outrage!'

'Of course you do. As Felicity said, you people have got networks, you always protect one of your own.' She laughed.

'Anyway,' she was fishing in her bag, 'I've got a little something for you. A leaving present from your boss.'

She handed Anna a piece of paper. 'You could have got more if you'd really fought, but I thought this would do for now.'

'Oh my God, Ruby, it's a cheque for £4,000.'

'And damned right too!'

'Oh Ruby, you're wonderful!' Anna flung her arms around her.

'I suppose I have my moments.'

Anna pulled her by the hand. 'Well, what are we waiting for? Let's get to the bank. I'm going to buy you something extravagant. Aah!' She pressed her hand to her side.

'Anna, what is it? Is it the baby?'

'I don't know, it hurts. I think it was when I pulled you. I'll be all right in a minute.'

'You're going straight home.' Ruby stepped into the road and yelled for a taxi.

'But what about your present? I want to get you something.'

'Anna, give me some credit. I'm not that grabby. I couldn't possibly drag you round the shops in pain.' She grinned at her. 'Anyway, you've got Andy's catalogues at home.'

Cass was already home when they got back and the doctor was on his way. Anna was resisting the fuss.

'It's okay. It was just a twinge. I'm fine now.'

The doctor, when he eventually arrived, agreed with her. 'Women get these things when they're pregnant,' he told Cass. 'You've got to remember that their hormones are going haywire. It's no surprise when some of them get hysterical. I've seen it time and again.'

Cass sneered at him as she shut the front door. 'Patronising bastard! I'd like to see him get a baby out of his arse. Then we'd have some fucking hysterics, you can be damned sure!'

Ruby smiled. 'Well, darling, charming as that idea is, I've got something in my bag that's going to make you feel even better. The best stress reliever in the world, and it's all yours.' She gave Cass the cheque. 'Money!'

Chapter 18

Drinks With Doris

When Ruby persuaded Johnnie and Shirley to join her for an evening with the Karloffs she deliberately didn't warn them about the illuminations. The night of the do itself was the night on which the Karloffs' grey stuccoed semi was transformed, with frightening vulgarity, into a Christmas theme park. On the stroke of six o'clock the switch was thrown, and the Close beheld the night of a thousand lights.

Shirley was coming down the stairs when it happened. Suddenly the hall was flooded with coloured light and the doorbell started ringing. She had a momentary panic about alien invasion and froze on the bottom step. Johnnie passed her, coming from his room. When he opened the door there was Ruby, silhouetted against a two-hundred-bulb snowman in the garden opposite.

'What the hell is going on?'

Ruby smiled. 'It's the spirit of Christmas, Karloff style. Don't you like it?'

'It's a monstrosity.' He went out into the road, shielding his eyes. 'And what the hell is on the roof?'

'That's Santa and his friendly helper the gift bunny.'

He looked back at her. 'I thought Santa had elves.'

'He does, but Sidney Prestwick is very fond of rabbits. Anna told me that their shed is full of them. She says there's at least forty of the things in there.' She sat on Greg's stone-clad front wall and waved to Shirley, who was still on the stairs. 'He's as mad as a biscuit.'

Shirley came out to join them. 'I think it's wonderful. The children around here must love it.'

'Yes, well,' Ruby was lighting a cigarette. 'Remember what happened to Hansel and Gretel. We don't call them Doris and Boris Karloff for nothing.'

They all looked at the gift bunny. Shirley was no longer sure that she wanted to go, but Johnnie was keener than ever.

'So what does he do with all his rabbits, then? I've never seen any.'

'They eat them.'

'Oh no!' Shirley was appalled. She thought about Henry the rabbit.

'Oh yes. Rabbit stew every Wednesday and a pair of extra warm slippers come Christmas.'

'That's terrible. They can't do that. We should ring the RSPCA.'

Ruby laughed. 'I'm joking. I don't know what he does with them. Maybe he sells them to pay for all the light bulbs.' She stubbed out her cigarette and started to cross the road. 'Just remember, when we go in, be careful where you tread.'

Ruby rang the bell and the front door opened before her finger had left the button. It was Doris, barely recognisable behind fifties make-up and a turquoise trouser-suit. She didn't smile but simply pointed towards a large plastic Santa, which beamed on the frosted glass door ahead. Shirley trailed behind Ruby and Johnnie, hoping that Greg would be there to make it all worthwhile.

Inside, the Karloffs' lounge was unbearably hot and unbearably red. The flock wallpaper, the shag pile carpet, the three-piece suite, everything was red. They had their gas fire on full blast and two portable electric bars positioned strategically to catch all unsuspecting ankles. The whole effect was more Satan's antechamber than Santa's grotto.

The others were already there, sweaty and uncomfortable. Greg, Cori and Cass were perched on the edge of the sofa, sipping sherry and cherryade. Anna had thrown decorum to the wind and was laid out, legs apart, on an armchair. Boris was hunched in another. Ruby laughed when she saw them.

'Happy Christmas, everyone! And what a swell party this is!' She wandered over to Anna. 'You look like you're enjoying yourself.'

Anna grimaced. 'Very funny. It wouldn't be so bad if I wasn't so blocked up.' She blew her nose noisily. 'And this is my only tissue. It's soaked.'

Doris's head poked out from behind Ruby's shoulder so suddenly that Anna jumped with shock.

'I'll take that.' She held out her hand for the tissue. 'Sidney will get you another one.'

She nodded pointedly at Boris, who shuffled out of the room. Anna held out her sodden scrap of loo-roll. Doris inspected it against the light, sniffed it and then tucked it away in the pocket of her trouser-suit. She smiled, pleased with herself, and left the room.

'Did you see that?' Anna hissed at Ruby. 'She's got my snot now.'

Ruby shrugged, lighting a cigarette. 'Did you want to keep it for yourself?'

'Of course not, Ruby. But I don't want her poking her fingers in it. She gives me the creeps. What do you think she's doing with it?'

'Making barbecue sauce?' Ruby laughed at Anna's serious face. 'I was joking.'

'Well, I'm not. She's probably mixing it with bats' eyes and slugs' breath.' She shuddered. 'This is definitely the last Christmas I'm doing this. I don't want anything more to do with them. I'm not even talking to them any more.'

She sat in sulky silence until Boris approached her with a tissue hanging over his index finger. 'For your dripping nose.'

Anna took it and smiled. 'Thanks very much, Sidney.'

He stepped back into the middle of the room, scanning the assembled faces. Ruby rolled her eyes and laughed loudly. 'Wow, you really socked it to him there, girl. Frightening!' She got up. 'Well, I'm off for an ashtray.' She held up her half-smoked cigarette. 'Let's see if Boris wants to have a good suck on my juices too.'

Boris had fixed his eyes on Shirley, who was sitting next to Cori on the sofa, talking about the decorations.

'I've never seen so many plastic Santas in one room. Have you, Cori?'

Boris took his chance. He swooped on them, squeezing himself between them on the sofa and placing his hand delicately on Shirley's knee.

'It's my collection. I like collecting things.' He smiled, curling strands of long greasy beard around his fingers. 'Some of my Santas are extremely valuable. Do you believe in Santa?'

Shirley shook her head, feeling the grip of Boris's hand inch up her leg.

'I've got the best ones in my workshop.'

'Really?' She looked urgently at Greg, but he was talking football with Johnnie.

'Why don't you come and have a look?'

'No, it's all right, thanks.'

'I think you'd like them. Do you like rabbits? I've got rabbits in my workshop. You can stroke one if you like.' He smiled, revealing a gold-filled front tooth. 'They like to be stroked.'

'Sorry, I'm allergic to rabbits.' Shirley knocked his hand off and fled to Ruby, who was disposing of her cigarette in a bucket-sized replica of Santa on his sleigh.

'I see Boris's introduced himself. Charming, isn't he?'

Shirley shuddered. 'He gives me the creeps. How long do we have to stay?'

'Not long. We'll wait until they've sung their Christmas duet, which is a treat not to be missed, and then it's off for a stiff drink at the Banana Cabaret.'

'I've got to wait for Mum and Dad. They're taking me home tonight.'

Ruby laughed. 'Ah, a cabaret of a different kind.'

'I'm really sorry about last week, Mum just bursting in like that. Thanks for letting her sleep in Johnnie's chair.'

'No problem, it was rather entertaining. And what about you, young Shirley? Anything happening with Greg?'

Shirley made patterns in the carpet with her foot. 'He's not interested in me. And anyway I don't like him anymore.'

'I see.' Ruby nodded, smiling. 'Of course I would have ignored that lie and called him over for a Christmas kiss, but I'm afraid you've missed your chance.'

Shirley turned around to see her dad beaming at them.

'Merry Christmas, everybody.'

Her mum was closed behind. 'Phew, is it warm in here or is it me?'

'It's warm.' Cass looked up from the sofa and Pearl sat down on the arm.

'Thank God for that, I thought I was having a hot flush. Anyway, how's the café? Any news?'

Cass shook her head. 'Not yet.'

'Oh well, I'm sure you'll get the money somehow.'

'Do you think so? I don't know how, not unless Santa drops it down the chimney.'

Pearl laughed. 'Forget it! He's a man, you can't rely on them for anything.' She waved to Ruby. 'Take it from one who knows.'

Shirley was whispering urgently in her mum's ear.

'Calm down, Shirley, we don't have to leave this minute. Do you remember Cass, Gordon? She works in the café we went to.'

'Oh, yes. Are you still serving that loofah?'

Shirley rolled her eyes. 'It's tofu, Dad.'

Cass smiled. 'We're not serving much at the moment. We're closing down. We can't get the investment we need.'

'Ah, well that's because people like meat, you see. It's all blacks and Asians around here, and you don't see them being vegetarian. You want to get some of that Halal stuff. That would bring them in.'

Cass bristled. 'Actually I'm half-Indian, and there are British-Caribbean and British-Asian members of our collective who are all vegetarian. Principles aren't race-related, Gordon.'

'Well, as my friend Keith always says to Lefties like you, the proof is in the profits. You see, without the customer base, only a fool would put his money into a venture like yours.'

Pearl glowered at him. 'Shut up, Gordon, you're not at the Gun and Gibbet now. Go and get me a sherry.' She turned to Cass. 'I'm sorry about Gordon. Sometimes I wonder what I ever saw in him.'

'It's okay, Pearl. Forget it.'

Shirley was hovering. 'Come on, Mum, I'll go without you if you don't come now!'

She stood by the door, waiting for her mother to get up, when suddenly it swung open, grazing her nose and revealing Doris standing just behind it with a full set of hand bells. Shirley froze in fright.

'You can't leave yet. We need you for the ding dong.'

Shirley backed into the lounge. 'Okay.' She glanced nervously at Cass.

Doris poked her with a pointed finger. 'You can be my helper. Make sure everyone has a bell.'

Shirley paled. 'Okay.' She started to pass the bells around. Cori clanged hers loudly and Greg shushed her.

Doris and Boris, meanwhile, had arranged themselves in front of the gas fire.

'It's now time for this year's ding dong. Please ring your bells.'

The din was dreadful. Without any rhythm or co-ordination the nine bells clanked and chimed. Amidst the noise, Doris and Boris began singing.

Ding dong merrily on high
On earth the bells are ringing
Ding dong verily the sky
In heaven the souls are singing

Glor-or-or-or-or-or-or
or-or-or-or-or-or
or-or-or-or-or-or
or-or-or-or-or-or
or-or-or-or-or-or-ia
Hosanna in excelsis

They all gave their bells back on the way out.

'Thank God that's over! Now let's escape the shadow of the gift bunny and go and have some fun.' Ruby waved her cabaret tickets at Cass and Anna. 'And I won't take no for an answer.'

Anna smiled. 'I wouldn't dare try.' She turned to Cass. 'Will you be wonderful to me and get my coat? It's just in the hall.'

Cass jogged next door. 'You take advantage of me, you do.' She reached the front door and gasped. 'Shit, fuck, shit!'

'Cass, what's the matter? What's happened?'

Anna ran to the house, with Ruby and Johnnie following. Cass gestured to their front door. Across the stained glass and old pine somebody had sprayed the words FUCK YOU DYKES.

Chapter 19

Shopping

'Come on, sweetie, let's burn plastic.'

Andy marched up to Cass, waving his credit card. It was wrapped in tinsel especially for their Christmas shopping trip. He skipped around her chanting, 'We're here, we're queer, we *are* going shopping. We're here, we're queer, we *are* going shopping.'

Cass was standing on the pavement but she wasn't ready and her smile was weary. Then Andy noticed the paintbrush in her hand.

Behind her the garden wall gleamed white. Beneath the fresh paint he could still read the words DEATH FOR DYKES scrawled across the bricks.

'Oh no, not again. When did this happen?'

Cass wiped the brush off.

'It must have been last night, I don't know when. I've been listening, you know, waiting for them, but I didn't hear a thing. I found it when I got up this morning. Anna's still in bed. It's going to freak her out when she sees it.'

'Well, let's not tell her.'

'Oh, what, just pretend I had a sudden desire to decorate? Yeah, right. She's really going to believe that.'

'This makes me so angry. Who the fuck is doing this?'

Cass shrugged. 'It could be anyone. It's probably someone we know.'

'That's so sick! Anna's a pregnant woman, for God's sake. This kind of stress is the last thing she needs.'

'Yeah, well, Ruby's coming over today, so she can keep her inside.'

Cass picked up the paint pot and Andy followed her into the house. The person who was watching them from the corner of the Close lit a cigarette.

When they reappeared Cass was dressed to go and the cigarette was long dead.

'It's the best therapy, believe me. We'll just leave all this crap behind and go and scandalise the elves.'

Cass grunted.

'Stop worrying! Anna is not going to come out here. She won't even know about it. Now who are we buying for?'

'Anna.'

'And?'

'Coriander.'

'And?'

'That's it. Anna's done everyone else. What about you?'

'Darling, I'd bought your presents in July. My only last-minute buy this year was Tony. I had to rush out in September when he came back to me.'

Cass managed a smile.

'Come on, sweetie, you know what I'm like, I love Christmas. As soon as Halloween's over I'm putting my tree up. November the fifth, you think bonfires, I think baubles.'

They walked hand in hand to the station.

'Tube or train?'

'Tube, then we can go for a coffee at First Out.'

The platform was heaving with people, but their pursuer was determined. She followed them into the carriage and kept up with them in the crowds getting off at Tottenham Court Road. She had them in sight right until the door of the café. Then she caught up and introduced herself.

'Hi, it's Andy, isn't it? You probably don't remember me. We met at Luigi's.'

Andy looked up.

'Of course I remember you, sweetie. You're the Angel of the hodgepodge.'

She smiled. 'Well, it needed saying. Trav told me that Anna had been sacked. I couldn't believe it.'

'That Granger woman's a bitch! But listen, where are my manners? This sulky person sitting here is Cass, Anna's partner.'

Cass smiled. 'Why not join us? We're about to have coffee.'

Angel sat down. 'Ta.'

Andy went up to the counter to order, and Angel started fiddling with the sugar bowl. Cass tried to make conversation. 'It was a bit of a night at Luigi's, then. I wish I'd been there.'

Angel didn't seem to hear. She tore open several packets of sugar and began pouring little piles on the table. Cass watched her, fascinated, as she swirled the sugar into a cartoon of Andy's face. When he came back Angel started talking.

'Look, I've got a confession. I didn't just bump into you here, right. I've been following you.'

Cass glanced nervously at Andy. 'What do mean "following"?'

Angel was still sculpting the sugar and didn't look up. 'From your house. I saw what had happened to the wall.'

'Hold on!' Cass reached across the table and put her hand over the sugar piles. 'Do you know something about who's doing this to us?'

Angel nodded. 'Yes. That's why I'm here.'

'So who is it?'

She studied the tablecloth. 'It's Trav.'

Cass stared at her. 'You're joking!' She stood up, tears springing in her eyes. 'Right! That fuckbrain is going to pay for what he's done! Fucking bastard, how could he do that to Anna?'

Andy grabbed her arm. 'Sit down, Cass.' He turned back to Angel. 'Did he tell you this?'

She shook her head. 'No, not in so many words.'

Cass was desperate. 'Is it him or not?'

Andy shushed her. 'Just let Angel tell us what she knows.'

Angel flattened the sugar and lit a cigarette.

'It's him all right! Look, a few days ago he started saying some nasty things about Anna. I mean he was well out of order. He took it really badly when she came out. He reckoned she'd led him on, made a fool of him, prick-teasing, stuff like that, ranting on. It was all crap, just homophobia, but I thought, well, so what if he's not perfect? We've all got hang-ups.' She made a face. 'I know that probably sounds crap to you. Anyway, I was wrong. He's a nasty, lying toe-rag and I never want to see him again. He told me he'd been all over the world, worked with Oxfam, done VSO in Africa, all that sort of stuff, but he's just a fucking con man.

'Last night he gets up, right, at two in the morning, and gets dressed. He thought I was asleep but I wasn't, and I saw him sneak out with this.' She pulled a used red spray can out of her bag. 'It's the same colour that's on your house, I checked this morning.' She gave it to Cass. 'And not only that. When he was out I went through his things. I don't normally do stuff like that, but I knew there was something going on. Anyway I found all these scrapbooks with letters in and stuff. So I read 'em.'

Cass took one of Angel's cigarettes. 'And?'

She grimaced. 'The man is well fucked up. He's, um, well in our relationship, he's got a problem, sexually you know, impotence. But I didn't mind that. I thought it was because he was so New Age and sensitive. Big joke that is. He was a bloody plumber in Melbourne until six months ago. I didn't know any of this until last night, but his wife left him two years ago for another woman. And my God, does he hate her! The things he was writing, it was scary stuff. He's really put her and this other woman through it. He thinks they've hexed him and taken away his manhood. Real self-pitying crap. I bet they were having a fucking party when he left for Britain.'

The coffees arrived and Angel gulped hers down.

'Anyway, he had Anna's address. It was all scribbled over and there were pictures of her and everything. When I saw that I got scared so I came to check it out. I saw you painting and then you came.' She nodded to Andy. 'When you went inside I was just thinking, Oh my God, I've been sleeping with a lying scheming reptile. I've got to dump him. Then I followed you.'

Cass leapt up. 'And now I'm going to fucking follow him.'

Andy stopped her again. 'And then what, Cass?'

Angel interrupted. 'Wait! It's worse than you think. You're not the only ones he's done this to. There's a whole list of others. He gets their numbers from the personals and sends them threats and stuff in the post. It's all written down. There's a whole folder of clippings. He's got a thing about humiliating gay women, making them scared. He gets off on it.'

Cass was raging. 'Cowardly shit!'

But Andy was calm. 'Angel, does he know that you know about him?'

'No, I left before he woke up.'

'Well, don't tell him. Dump him, but don't tell him why.'

Cass glared at them. 'And then what? He can't just get away with this.'

'Then we'll meet and we'll plot. You tell Anna, Cass, and let me speak to Tony. When we get this weasel, we'll do it with style, not force. I've got an idea.'

Chapter 20

Christmas Dinner

Starters

'No, Shirley, you can't come in. I'm not finished yet.'

'Oh, come on, Mum. You've been in there ages.' Shirley leant against the dining-room door, but it wouldn't open more than a crack. Something was blocking it. 'Please, Mum, Dad's making me watch the panto again.'

It was a plea for solidarity. The golf club's Christmas panto-mime was an annual ordeal for mother and daughter alike. Gordon was chair of the club's entertainment committee and family loyalty was imperative. They had already sat through the live performance of *Cinderella: Or You Need Balls to Get Birdies.* Now they were enduring the edited highlights. They could both hear Keith Smedley's hilarious antics as the back end of the pantomime horse. Gordon called out.

'Quick, Shirley, you're missing that bit with the salami.'

Her mum took pity on her. 'Alright then. But remember it's not finished yet. So you won't get the full effect.'

There was a shuffling as Pearl rolled the hostess trolley away from the door. It had been a present from Gordon, but as far as Shirley could see her mum only ever used it as a barricade. Pearl opened the door with a flourish.

'Da dah!'

Shirley looked at the dining room table in silence. Her mother prompted her.

'I've taken holly as my central theme.'

'I can see that.'

'It's taken me weeks of work.'

The table was festooned with holly leaves: real ones, painted ones, embroidered ones. They were appliquéd to the tablecloth, stencilled on to the plates, even the glasses had holly in them. Shirley's immediate thought was that her mother was a woman with too much time on her hands.

'On the plates, darling, that's edible gold leaf so it doesn't matter if it comes off on the food.'

Pearl went over to the teak-effect sideboard.

'And this is my *pièce-de-résistance*, my centrepiece for the whole ensemble. What do you think?'

Shirley didn't know what to say. Her mother was holding up a plate wrapped in black crêpe paper. There was a bare-bone turkey carcass on it, which had been painted gold and stuffed with silver tinsel. The whole thing was tied up with a black ribbon and surrounded by satsumas.

Her mother looked at her expectantly.

'I'm calling it "The Ghost of Christmas Past". I did it at the Art Circle.'

She put the turkey on the table and reached for the cutlery. Knives first.

'We got rid of old Olive Hargreaves, you know. Gave her the boot. Well, every week it was the same with her, church views and tulips in a pot. I mean, I'm not interested in graveyard scenes, I have enough of that at home.'

Then the forks.

'Now we've got Lucasta teaching us. Oh, she's prodded them into life, all right. You wouldn't recognise that group since she's taken over. The things we do now, she's an inspiration to me.'

Finally spoons.

'She wants us to scoop out our souls and produce art from within. I've discovered a whole new side to myself.'

Shirley looked at the bizarre thing on the table and wondered whether her mother's insides weren't best left alone.

'I can see by your face you don't like it, Shirley.'

'It's not that, Mum.' Shirley tried to be tactful. 'It's just that we normally have a vase of flowers or something.'

'You don't like it because you don't understand it. It's like Lucasta says to our Circle, the best art cannot always speak for itself. It sometimes needs help.'

She looked seriously at her daughter.

'You see, Shirley, that turkey is me, you and your father.'

She paused, staring at it. Shirley was clenched with the effort not to giggle.

'What I see when I look at my piece on that table is the death of how we were as a family. Things aren't the same now. You've moved out, you don't need me any more. It's just the two of us. Of course, it might have been different if we could have had more children, but that wasn't to be.'

She shifted the carcass slightly to the side and straightened the ribbon.

'Lucasta says I'm just beginning to find my artist's eye. She's told us all at the Circle that we've got to start expressing ourselves and not just seeing everyone else's needs. So I'm starting with Christmas. No more turkey, no tinsel, no satsumas.'

Shirley had stopped laughing. 'No turkey?'

'If you want turkey, you can cook it yourself.'

'It's too late for that now.'

'Well, for the first year ever, you'll have to eat what I want, won't you?'

'And what's that, then?'

Pearl smiled. 'Wait and see. Go and tell your father it's ready.'

Shirley went to get her dad, who was cracking walnuts in the lounge.

'Nut, Shirley?'

'No thanks, dinner's ready.'

'Good-oh.' Gordon tucked the nutcrackers into the handi-pocket on his armchair and got up.

'Listen, Dad, I don't know what's wrong with Mum, but she's gone mad with the tablecloth and we're not having turkey for dinner. I'm warning you now because I don't want a row when we're eating. Just try not to say anything.'

Gordon had stopped listening at the mention of no turkey. 'What are we having then, partridge, pheasant, goose?'

'I'm not sure.' Shirley had a sinking feeling about the whole thing. 'I'll go and ask Mum.'

She glanced into the kitchen as her dad went into the dining room. Her mum was getting a tureen out of the fridge. Things didn't look hopeful. She went back to join him.

When he saw the table he looked confused.

'I thought you said it was ready? Your mother's not even finished clearing up in here. Get the dustpan, Shirley.'

'No, Dad, the leaves are supposed to be there. The table is on a holly theme.'

Gordon was emptying the leaves out of the glasses. 'What do you mean *theme*? We can't eat like this. We'll do ourselves an injury. It's a recipe for indigestion.' He started scraping leaves on to the floor. 'That's if we don't get poisoned. How can I carve a turkey on this?'

'We're not having turkey.'

'We're not having anything in this mess.' Something caught his eye. 'What the hell is that?'

He was pointing at the carcass.

'It's the centrepiece. Mum did it at the Art Circle.'

'Art Circle? It looks like something from the bin. What's going on here?'

They contemplated it in silence. Shirley started to giggle. They looked at each other.

'Is she taking lessons from that Hearse fellah now?'

'It's Hirst, Dad. Damien Hirst.'

'Yes, well. We should show him that thing. He could put it in a gallery at the taxpayer's expense.' He saw Pearl come in with the dinner but he was enjoying himself. 'He and your mother could set up shop together. What do you think of this, Shirley, "Damned Hearse meets Pearly Gates".'

They were both laughing as Pearl put the tureen on the table and sat down. She waited until they had stopped before serving.

'Here we are, you two. We're having something different this Christmas.' She lifted the lid. 'Sushi.'

Main

Anna was tense. 'Okay, can everyone sit down please? Cass is about to bring in the nut roast.'

Andy waved a cracker at her but she ignored him. She put potatoes on the table and went back to the kitchen for sprouts. She was tense about Tony. Greg and Andy were already sitting at the table, wearing paper hats, but Tony hadn't moved from the sofa. He was playing Barbie and Ken with Coriander.

'You can be Ken, and I'll be Barbie.' Cori gave him a doll, then reconsidered. 'But you can be Barbie if you like.'

Greg laughed. 'Wow, you are honoured. I never get to be Barbie.'

Cori put her hand on her hip. 'That's because Tony's better at being a girl.'

Greg looked embarrassed. 'Cori, come and sit down here. Dinner's ready.'

'No, Daddy. Me and Tony and Barbie and Ken are eating here.' She pointed to the coffee table. 'Barbie and Ken have asked us.'

'Yes, well, Anna and Cass have asked you too.' He gestured for her to sit next to him.

'It's okay, Greg. She can eat down there.' Anna put the sprouts on the table in front of him. 'She doesn't have to sit with us if she doesn't want to.'

'Tony doesn't want to sit with you, either. He told me.'

There was a momentary silence. Anna glanced at Andy. 'That's all right, darling. Tony can sit with you and your dolls.'

Cori turned to Tony, pleased with herself. 'You're my new friend. You call me Barbie and I'll call you Ken.'

Greg looked to Anna. 'Sorry about that.' Andy said nothing.

Cass was at the door. 'Fanfare please. Here's my Christmas speciality. Cashew nut roast with sherry and mushroom sauce.'

Anna smiled. 'Looks delicious.' There was general murmuring of appreciation.

'Okay, let's get stuck in. Pass up your plates.' Cass looked at Tony and Coriander. 'Are we not all sitting at the table?'

Anna made light. 'Poor Tony's been pressganged into playing Ken. He's eating over there with Barbie.'

'Oh well, as long as he doesn't mind, I'm sure we'll cope without him.' Cass smiled to herself as she served up the roast.

Anna caught Andy's eye. 'God, what are we thinking of? There's no music! It's just not Christmas without some slushy old crooner on the go.'

Cass groaned. 'Not bloody Bing Crosby again!'

Anna threw a cracker at her. 'Naff off Ebenezer, it's Christmas! Anyway, it's not Bing Crosby, it's Dean Martin.' She turned up the volume. 'And it's a classic, so don't even think of turning it off.'

Greg took his plate from Cass. 'It's a shame Ruby couldn't make it.'

'She didn't want to come. Anna asked her. She's always like this at Christmas. I think Johnnie's going to hers later, if he can get away from his family.'

'You'd have thought Ruby would love Christmas.'

Anna gave him some sprouts. 'She's just not into Christmas Day, that's all. She's got her reasons. Anyway, let's have a toast. What shall we toast to?'

'To friendship.' Greg clinked her glass.

'And the chef.' Anna raised her glass to Cass.

Cass found her wine and touched it to Anna's glass. 'And to great big bellies.'

'And wonderful new families.' Andy laughed, clattering all their glasses with the bottle.

Tony stayed silent on the sofa.

Dessert

Johnnie was lying on his back across the mess of sheets on Ruby's bed. She was sitting above him and he gently stroked her thighs as she fed him another Belgian chocolate.

'Am I ever glad I found you, Ruby.'

She smiled distractedly and bent her head to his dark chest, kissing each nipple.

'I got you a present.' He lifted her, bringing her face to his own, and then rolled her over, pressing his weight against her belly and breasts. 'Stay there.' He leapt off the bed and started to rummage among the piles of their clothes, looking for his jacket. Ruby lit a cigarette.

'You know I didn't get you anything. I don't really do this present thing.'

Johnnie smiled at her and climbed back on the bed, hiding something in his fist.

'Ruby, you've given me champagne, chocolate, cannabis and cunt. It's the best Christmas present a man could ever have.'

'I'm glad you liked it.' She turned to find the ashtray. 'But please lay off the c word.'

Johnnie laughed. 'Okay, you'll get no more cunt from me.'

'Not that. I'm talking about Christmas.'

'What, you don't like Christmas? I don't believe you. Everyone loves Christmas.'

'Well, not me.'

'What about when you were a kid? All kids love Christmas.'

'Look, can we just leave it?'

He put his hands up in mock defeat, but her mood had changed. She slammed both fists on to the bed.

'Why is everyone always on about fucking Christmas as if it's so fucking great?'

Johnnie was confused and subdued by the force of her anger. 'Well, I know Christmas is commercialised crap, but it's fun too.'

Ruby was brooding, biting her lip.

'I wish you'd have come with me today and met my folks. Christmas is great with them, you'd have loved it.'

She looked at him as if he were a child playing with childish things. He took a risk. He opened his hand.

There was a brightly wrapped small box on his palm. To Ruby the joke seemed so inappropriate that it made it funny again. She smiled. Johnnie was holding a ring box.

'Don't tell me, you got me something every girl longs for.'

He was relieved to hear that teasing edge back in her voice, but his heart still beat stubbornly fast against his chest.

'And, let me guess, it's small and round and gold.'

She was enjoying herself. Hoped surged through him.

'I've got it. It's a Ferrero Roché.' He laughed. 'No, it's little gold nipple warmers for these cold winter months, or perhaps even better a . . .'

He stopped her, unable to bear the waiting.

'Open it.'

He thought she was teasing him, but she was just enjoying his joke. The irreverence was perfect. A perfect joke on the spirit of Christmas. It simply did not occur to her that it might be anything else.

She opened it. A single ruby rested on a gold band. Like blood on skin. Her shock was physical.

Johnnie was anxious. 'Do you like it? I fell for it as soon as I saw it. Just like I fell for you.' It was a prepared line that didn't come out as he'd hoped. Ruby's face was like stone. 'But when you're asking Ruby Gold to marry you, you have to do it with style. So what do you say?'

He was speaking into an unnatural silence. Not the silence of surprise or delight, or even simple rejection.

'I know this is sudden, Ruby, but it's real. I want to spend my life with you. I love you and I want you to be my wife.'

When she finally spoke, the words sounded strange and sluggish in her mouth.

'Get out!'

He blinked, thinking he'd misheard her. She didn't look up.

'Get out, get out, get out.' It was a mantra building to a scream. She held the words like a fierceness between her teeth and threw herself at him, biting and shrieking. He fell backwards on to the floor and she ripped at his face with her nails, cutting his cheek and neck. He lashed out, trying to get hold of her arms but she pulled away and fell roughly against the bed. She collapsed against the frame, slicing her hand on the broken ashtray. The shock of the pain stunned her. Then she began sobbing, sobbing and choking and shouting, but not at Johnnie. He watched from the doorway as Ruby lost herself to the ghosts of her past.

Chapter 21

Ruby's Story

Ruby was quiet. Johnnie moved towards her and sat close to where she was crouching beside the bed. He didn't dare touch her. He looked around at the mess of the room and at the blood still dripping slowly from her hand. She spoke without looking up.

'Why are you here, Johnnie?'

'Because I couldn't leave you like this.' He tried to lift her hair away from her face but she shook him off.

'I don't just mean now. I mean why are you fucking a white woman old enough and fat enough to be your mother?'

'Don't talk like that, Ruby.'

'Why not? That's the truth.'

'No, it's not. I'm with you because I love you.'

'Yeah, so you said.'

They were silent again. Ruby squeezed her hand, making the blood ooze down her arm.

'If you want to fuck your mother why don't you just go home and do it?'

Johnnie tensed, clenching his fists. 'Why are you doing this, Ruby?'

'Because I'm not going to be your big white mammy.'

'Who the fuck asked you to be?'

'You did.'

'I asked you to be my wife. There's a difference.'

'I'm not being anyone's wife.' Sobs were welling up in her throat. 'I look after myself. Nobody's going to crush me and call it love.'

'I'm not going to crush you, Ruby.' Johnnie took her in his arms and she broke down.

'I won't love you, I can't.'

'Shush, it's okay.'

'I can't feel love any more.'

'Don't worry, don't talk now.'

Ruby whispered into his shoulder.

'She was exactly my age.'

He stroked her hair. 'Who was, babe?'

'When she died, she was exactly my age.'

'Who died, Ruby?'

'She did. He killed her.' She spoke in a hesitant, childlike tone. 'We had the same birthday. When I was little we'd blow out the candles holding hands. I used to open her cards.'

He could feel her tears rolling silently down his back.

'Ruby,' he lifted her head to see her face, 'are you talking about your mum?'

She closed her wet eyes and bit hard on trembling lips.

'When did she die, Ruby?'

She sniffed. 'It was a long time ago.'

'Were you a child?'

She shook her head. 'No.'

Johnnie was trying to make sense of what had happened, guessing parts of her story before she could tell them. 'Did she die on Christmas Day?'

Ruby looked at him and nodded. 'He killed her.'

'On Christmas Day?'

She spoke as if all feeling had left her. 'He killed her and I couldn't help her. I was too skinny and weak, trying to be Kate Bush.' She tried to smile. 'The police didn't come until she was already dead. They wouldn't let me stay with her. The ambulance took me away.'

'Were you hurt too?'

'She was dead.'

She didn't want to talk any more. Johnnie gave her a cigarette and she smoked it in silence. He went downstairs to get some brandy. When he came back Ruby had begun to tidy up. He put down the glasses.

'Hey, leave that, I'll do it.'

'It's okay. I'm better now. I'm so sorry for what I did to your face.' She stroked his cheek.

'Forget it, it's just a scratch. Your hand is much worse. We should bandage it.'

'No, it's stopped bleeding. Leave it now, I want to explain.'

'There's no need, babe.'

'There is for me.'

They sat on the bed and he gave her a brandy. Ruby took a sip.

'It was twenty years ago that it happened. At the dinner table. Just after plum pudding and cream.' She gave Johnnie an ironic smile. 'He came in, you see, drunk. He'd been on some kind of bender and slept rough.' She rolled the brandy around her glass.

'He was angry because we'd eaten without him. He said he'd got her a present, a metal statuette thing that he'd probably robbed out of some house. It wasn't wrapped. I remember it clearly from the trial. It was a bronze figurine of an eighteenth-century lady and her dog. At first he just slammed it on the table to make us move, to frighten us into getting his dinner. But I made her stay. I told him that if she got up, it would be to leave him for good, and that I'd make sure she did.

'I wasn't living there by then, I'd left years before. I'd tried to make her come with me, but she wouldn't. He would have come after us, you see, and blamed me. She protected me with her body, letting him take out his rages on her, not me. And I let her do it.

'Anyway, it was the wrong time to make a stand. He didn't even try to argue or shout. He just smacked her in the face with that statue and then smacked me. It was that first blow to the head that killed her. The coroner said it was pretty much instant, but neither of us knew that then. I crawled out of the house to get help. He just kept battering her and she was already dead.'

She drained her glass and held it out for more.

'Afterwards it was the same as it always was. He held her in his arms and begged forgiveness. Told her how much he loved her and that it was only love that made him get so mad. He was asking forgiveness from a corpse. That's how he was when the police got there.'

Johnnie gave her another brandy and she gulped it back.

'He got a life sentence and five more years for what he did to me.' She lit a cigarette. 'I hope he's slowly rotting to death.'

Johnnie didn't know what to say. He wasn't going to tell Ruby that if he wasn't dead, her father was probably out of prison already. If she didn't know, it was because she didn't want to. They sat in silence, not touching. And then suddenly Ruby got up.

'There's something I want to show you.'

She went over to her dresser and picked up a carved wooden box.

'My mother's jewellery box.'

There wasn't much inside. A large silver brooch, some glass beads in different colours, a hat pin. Ruby found a scrap of blue tissue paper and took it out.

'I want you to see this, because I want you to understand. And then I want you to go, Johnnie. I don't want to hurt you, but I don't love you. And don't think I'm just saying this because I'm emotionally damaged, I don't need you to heal me. I don't need love, and I don't want it. It's my choice.' She gave the package to Johnnie. 'I think that after today, it's best if we stop seeing each other. And please don't make it worse for me by outstaying your welcome.'

Johnnie unwrapped the tissue paper

'That was her engagement ring.'

He stood up and walked out the door. The ring was still on the bed where he'd left it. A gold band with a single ruby.

Chapter 22

Revenge

The Prince Edward was heaving. It was New Year's Eve and the karaoke show was in full swing. John Lennon and Yoko Ono were sitting on the stage in sleeping bags, waving 'Bed-In for Peace' placards to 'All You Need is Love'. Anna watched them briefly from the corner of the pub as she scanned the room, searching the faces in the swaying crowds. She was looking for Trav and at the same time dreading finding him. It was hard to face her tormentor. Harder still to accept how much he must hate her. Angel was bringing him to them tonight, a politically correct Judas, betraying the betrayer. It was the first stage in their plan.

A crowd of flower children were pushing through the bouncers, giving them plastic rifles with pansies in the ends. This year The Prince Edward was recycling New Year (all proceeds to Greenpeace). After the futurist excesses of the millennium, this New Year's Eve was decidedly retro. Over the stage a psychedelic banner told them to 'Say Goodbye to 1969'.

Anna turned back to Andy. 'There's still no sign of them. What if Angel's changed her mind and they're not coming?'

Andy leaned over from the *chaise-longue*, his worry beads

draping into her lap. 'Sweetie, relax, you're stressing.' He puffed on his massive fake joint and held it out to her. She shook her head. 'Not for smoking, you silly, lesbian person. It's cotton wool! Give it a squeeze. It's therapeutic.' She took it and stuck it back on to his hatband.

He was wearing a Texan hat, a long-haired wig, and an over-sized poncho (his spare pink blanket). He called it his Cape Horn look. Anna had on Janis Joplin hair, feathers and glasses with a tie-dyed maternity dress that was a present from Sky. Across the front it said 'Mother Nature Made My Baby'. Sky had embroidered it herself.

'Listen, sweetie, Angel said she'd bring Trav, and she will. Now, finish your drink. Daisy and Polly are finalising the plan.'

Daisy and Polly (stars of club cabaret as Upsa Daisy and Polly Morphous-Perversity) were sitting on the other side of Andy on the *chaise-longue*. They were both immaculate. Plucked, tweaked and painted to perfection. Daisy was a dead ringer for Diana Rigg in *The Avengers* and Polly, white-lipped and spider-eyed, a perfect Mary Quant. Sitting with them in her embroidered tent and feathers, Anna felt like a badly stuffed parrot. She glanced at Cass, who was wearing a short blonde wig and yellow hotpants and chatting excitedly to Daisy. She looked like a ten-year-old boy flirting with someone's mother. Anna felt a lot better.

Greg and Ruby were sitting on the other side of Cass, on a narrow wooden settle. It was part of The Prince Edward's collection of old furniture, now shoved into corners to make space for the stage. Ruby was perched next to Greg, making an ostentatious show of only fitting half her buttocks on the seat.

'God, didn't they have bottoms in the nineteenth century? I've never sat on anything so uncomfortable, and that includes bendy Kevin.'

Anna laughed. 'Oh yes, Bananaman. I'd forgotten about him.'

Ruby got off the settle and looked down at it.

'I mean, I've seen wider railings. Are you sure it's not a shelf?' She crouched down and sat cross-legged on the floor next to Anna's chair. 'Ignore me then, everyone, I'll just crawl in the dirt.'

Andy was moving beer mats across the table until they surrounded a box of matches. He plonked a lighter on top of it. 'And that's when we jump him.'

Anna looked from the lighter to the door, squinting through the crowds. Ruby pulled on her dress.

'Stop worrying and talk to me! No one's even looked at me tonight. If I'd known we were launching a military campaign, I'd have worn khaki.'

Anna rolled her eyes. 'Shut up, Ruby, it's hardly Kosovo! Anyway you look much better in black. Is that dress an original?' Anna felt the silver beadwork on Ruby's sleeve.

'It was my mother's.'

'Oh, Ruby, I . . .'

'It's okay, Anna. I don't want to talk about it, I just wanted to wear it.'

Anna was quiet. She was thinking about Johnnie. Ruby looked at her as she lit a cigarette. 'I know what you're thinking and he's old news.' She took a drag. 'It's been a week already, I'm completely over him. In fact, I'm hoping for a bit of action tonight.' She leant on her elbow and looked out across the carpet. 'Somewhere in that maze of legs, there's a man in an afghan just waiting for my nirvana.' She sighed dreamily. 'Anyway, who are you supposed to be?'

'Janis Joplin. What do you think of my feathers?' She shook her head and let them drape across her face. 'Cass hates them.'

'I should think so, if this were really 1969 you'd be dead soon.'

Andy was calling for their attention. 'So we're all agreed on "What's New Pussycat"?'

Daisy took a match out of the box on the table and held it up. 'See that, girls.' She looked at Greg. 'Oh sorry, we've got a real man with us, haven't we? See that, Greg?' She smiled winningly in his direction. Greg blushed wildly, mumbling something to his beer. Daisy kicked him playfully with her thigh boot. 'Aren't you just the cutest man?'

Polly slapped her. 'Down, girl! Stick to the match.'

'Oh yes, this match, darlings,' Daisy waved in front of them, 'is the scumbag Travis, and this . . .' she said, lighting it with a flourish, 'is what we pussycats are going to do to him when we get on that stage.'

Anna held Ruby's hand. 'I'm so nervous! What if he doesn't fall for it?' She looked back into the crowd. Trav was there, standing just yards away in jeans and a buckskin waistcoat. 'Oh my God, he's here! Andy, he's here! He's here, everyone! Oh my God!'

Andy shushed her. 'It's okay, Anna. We're ready for him. Greg, you go with Cass. Polly and Daisy, you start on him at the bar. I'll sort things out back here.'

Cass blew a kiss to Anna as she put her arm through Greg's. They sauntered over to the bar with Daisy and Polly behind them, cooing over Greg's bottom. Ruby watched them go. Greg was wearing Johnnie's T-shirt and 'Are you experienced?' flashed at her through the crowd. She lowered her eyes and turned back to Anna.

'I hate being left on the sidelines.'

'You have to be, Ruby, Trav's met you, remember?'

'Yes, I know, I know. But if it wasn't for that I could have starred in this. I could've seduced that prat with my eyes closed.'

Andy moved up to be next to them. 'They'd have to be, he's an ugly git.'

'I mean, what's Daisy got that I haven't?'

Andy laughed. 'Two heads?'

Ruby looked confused. 'You mean? No!' She looked at Anna. 'Daisy's got a dick? Oh my God, they're men, aren't they?'

Anna nodded. 'Of course they are. God, Ruby, where have you been? They've got queer stamped all over them.'

'Have they?' Ruby looked back to the bar. 'They seemed normal to me.'

Andy was taking the drinks off the table. 'Of course they do, Ruby. Now stand up.'

'What are you doing with that table?'

Andy squeezed past her. 'Moving it. It's all part of the plan.'

Anna squinted up at her, shielding her eyes from the glitter-ball. 'You haven't been listening at all, have you?'

Ruby lit a cigarette. 'Well, I wasn't in it, was I? It was boring.'

Anna humphed. 'You are unbelievable! Now listen up, and listen good.'

Over at the bar, Cass and Angel had staged bumping into each other and were hugging like old friends.

Angel held Cass by the shoulders. 'It's so good to see you again. I can't believe it! Happy New Year!'

'Happy New Year to you!' Cass was struggling with unexpected giggles.

Angel steered her around so Trav couldn't see. 'So are you going to introduce us to your friends? This is Trav, by the way.' She pointed behind her. Trav was staring at Polly and she smiled sweetly back. Angel winked at Cass. He was taking the bait.

Cass bit her lip. 'This is my boyfriend, Greg.' Greg nodded at them stiffly. 'And my friends Daisy and Polly.' They air-kissed first Angel then Trav.

Cass nudged Greg in the ribs. 'Drinks, Greg.'

'Oh yes. What's everyone having?'

'I'll find us a table.' Cass ran back to Anna. 'Okay, we're coming over, time to hide.'

Andy had pulled out the settle and Cass helped them crawl in behind it. Ruby moaned loudly. 'This is ridiculous! Do we have to hide behind this? It was bad enough sitting on it.'

Andy pushed her in. 'If we don't, we won't hear what's said. We'll miss all the fun.'

'Well, I'm already missing the feeling in my feet. Crouching is not something I do without a big incentive behind me.'

Andy laughed. 'Ruby, are you sure you're not a gay man?'

She winked at him. 'Call me Rubin.'

Cass knocked on the wood and shushed them. 'They're coming.'

Greg put the drinks down on the table and sat next to Cass on the settle. He nodded to Angel, pointing surreptitiously to a pint of lager on the tray. While Polly flirted with Trav behind her, Angel took the glass and spiked it with a slug of vodka from a bottle in her bag. Silently, she showed the others how much had gone. Daisy watched carefully, waiting until the bottle was out of sight before grabbing Trav and pulling him down between her and Polly on the *chaise-longue*.

'So,' Daisy pouted. 'Is it Trav or Travis?'

Polly giggled. 'I love that name. It's so hunky.'

'Well, girls,' Trav winked and held them by the knee, 'as I say when I'm travelling, names are just words. It's people that matter in this world.'

Behind the settle, Andy stuck his fingers down his throat.

'Do you travel a lot, Travis?'

'Daisy, you probably can't understand this, but travelling is my life. It's in my blood. Not even a beautiful woman like you could make me settle down in one place.'

She blew her smoke slowly into his face. 'So you're a "wham, bam, thank you ma'am" are you?'

His top lip curled into a smile and he picked up his drink. 'When I've been with a woman, Daisy, she thanks me.'

Girlish giggling broke through cries of 'You are awful' and 'That's so sexist.' Daisy and Polly were edging closer.

'So, Travis, tell us about your travels.'

He took a deep swig from his lager.

'Have you girls ever been to Quamquat? It's a little village just outside of Lima in Peru. No? That's a pity, because in that village there's a wise man who only speaks once a year. His name is Hari-annual. I was there in that village on the precise day he was gonna talk. And do you know what, he saw me in the crowd and he looked into my eyes and he beckoned me over with his finger. Just like this, Daisy. He said, get closer, closer, closer, until I was nose to nose with him, just like I am with you, babe. Nose to nose. And then do you know what he said to me? Do you wanna know the truth? I'll tell you if you kiss me.'

Daisy giggled and pecked him on the cheek.

'That's not a kiss.'

He turned to Polly. 'Do you wanna know what he said?'

She leant forward and kissed him slowly, openly and with

plenty of tongue. Trav smiled at her. 'Do you wanna know the truth? I'll tell you if you kiss me.'

Polly pouted. 'I just did.'

He turned back to Daisy.

'What about you, darlin'?'

Daisy grabbed the back of his head and drew him towards her. She parted his teeth with her tongue and rammed it home. Trav came away sucking his cheeks.

'Whoah! That's some kiss you got, Daisy.'

'So tell me what he said, then.'

'Do you wanna know the truth? I'll tell you if you kiss me.' He started to laugh. 'That's what he said, girls. The old guru was a homo. So I said to him, I don't kiss men for all the bloody money in China. You can keep your truth, you poofter. He didn't expect that, you see. They say he hasn't spoken since.' He smiled proudly. 'Now you don't get stories like that when you sit on your arse at home.'

Cass clapped. 'Hey, Trav, if you've travelled so much I bet you've seen real karaoke in Japan then?'

They were talking over the growls of a female trio singing 'Big Spender'.

'Seen it? God, girl, you don't just watch karaoke in Japan. If you don't join in, they bloody have you.'

'So you've done it before then?'

'Only about a hundred times. I bummed my way round Japan getting free meals in karaoke bars, you know.' He turned back to Polly. 'That's a little trick I share with the student travellers that come into my bookshop. I tell them, if you're going to sell yourself out there, sell your voice, not your arse. You'll get more.' He laughed and hit the table. 'Especially with some of the fat arses on them.'

Polly squeaked. 'Oh, you'll have to do karaoke for us.'

'Oh yes,' Daisy was stroking his arm. 'It'd be awesome.'

Polly sat on his lap. 'Please, Trav. You've got me all excited now.' She looked wide-eyed at Daisy. 'I know, why don't we come up with you? We could be your chorus girls.'

'Or your dancers.' They both giggled and Polly pressed her

finger to her cheek, tilting her head to one side. 'Now what shall we sing?'

'I know.' Daisy was bouncing on her seat. ' "What's New Pussycat?"'

'Oh yes, yes.' Polly started bouncing too. 'It's my favourite.'

Trav had his arms around both of them, shaking his head. 'Sorry, girls. Not tonight.'

Angel got up, smiling. 'No way, Trav! You can't back out now. I'm putting your names down.'

It wasn't long before Terry the MC called them over. Angel went up with them to make sure Trav didn't back out. Terry was another friend of Andy's.

'And now we have Travis as Tom Jones with his lovely dancers, Polly and Daisy.'

A huge cheer went up as the girls walked on stage. They had a big following in the straight pubs. The music started.

> *What's new pussycat?*
> *Oh woh-woh-woh-woh-woh*
> *What's new pussycat?*
> *Oh woh-woh-woh-woh-woh-woh.*

Trav froze to the spot with the microphone in his hand. The girls 'oh-woh-wohed' up and down the sides of his body, trying to stir him into action. Daisy cast a worried glance at Terry, who turned up the backing track. At last Trav began to sing. A strained squeak struggled from his throat and raced on several beats too fast. Polly and Daisy smiled into the audience and set to work. By the end of the first chorus Daisy had his waistcoat off. She twirled it over her head and threw it into the crowd. Polly laughed at his protestations and kissed him.

'Keep singing, sexy. I love a hairy chest.'

Trav read off the screen.

> *'You and your pussycat eyes, ooh.'*

Polly was kneeling in front of him now, rubbing his chest. Daisy was behind him with a pair of nail scissors. She grabbed the back of his jeans and started cutting. Once through the belt she left a few threads of the waistband intact to hold them up and then carved down the line of his buttocks. His stage fright was perfect. Never had Tom Jones thrusted less. At the back of the pub, Andy was leading the others through the crowd.

The final chorus. Daisy and Polly were swaying either side of Trav with their hands on the sides of his trousers. As the last few chords blared from the karaoke, Daisy took the mike. 'Travis, darling, this is a little surprise for you from Anna who's here tonight with all her friends. It's called revenge.'

In one movement they yanked at his trousers with one hand, and their wigs with the other. Travis stood there with his jeans rounds his ankles, holding two men in his arms. The whole place exploded with laughter and applause. Andy, Cass, Ruby, Greg, Angel and Anna burst through the curtains on the back of the stage, whooping with delight. Cass took the mike.

'We'd like to dedicate this act of cabaret vengeance to Anna and all the other women out there who've been harassed by cowardly knobheads like him.'

Travis grabbed for his pants and crawled off the stage into the crowd. They parted before him like the Red Sea, clapping, cheering and jeering him all the way to the door. On stage Polly, now a red-lipped Liza Minnelli, began to sing the opening lines of *Cabaret*.

Cass helped Anna off the stage. 'What did you think? Good, wasn't it?'

'Good? It was wonderful, I feel fantastic.' She put her hand over her stomach. 'And the baby's been doing somersaults.'

'He'll think twice about messing with us again.' Cass knelt down. 'And you, my little one. You get any trouble at school, and we'll get Daisy on to it.'

Chapter 23

The Play

Pearl and Gordon were late. Shirley was hanging on the stage door, waiting for them to arrive. She looked over to where Iain was sitting with the cash box at the other end of the foyer. If her parents didn't come soon, she'd have to leave their tickets with him. She willed them to walk through the door. She'd been avoiding Iain since the party.

Gail poked her head out of the door behind her and called her back into the green room (aka Lecture Theatre B). It was a bleak teaching room with a side door to Lecture Theatre A, the main stage. They were all being assessed on tonight's performance for their module in Dramatic Production. Rob, their tutor, was sitting on a table at the front, swinging his legs and scribbling on a clipboard. He winked at Nigel, the director, who was gathering everyone together.

'Listen up, people. Can we all come to the front please? And just ignore Rob, okay.'

There was a mumbling of predictable jokes about how they did anyway, especially in his lectures. Shirley ran down the steps to join the group.

'Are we all with me? Okay, let's become a circle. Now, people,

just breathe. We're breathing in energy. We're breathing in con-
fidence. And now we're sighing away negativity, we're expelling
anxiety. Okay, Geraldine?'

The leading lady had a reputation as a vomiter. Shirley
exhaled loudly.

'Okay, now swing.' They all swung their arms. 'And I want
to see smiling.' Flashes of nervous teeth. Remember, we've done
this as a team. We've written it, created it, made it happen. Let's
open this show with a bang.'

He punched the air and they all whooped. Nigel shouted over
the noise.

'And before you all go on I just want to say, I'm so proud of
you. I think you're all bloody fantastic.'

His mobile phone was ringing to the tune of Beethoven's
Fifth. He held up his arms to quieten them. 'People, while I get
this, just give yourselves a great big bloody hug.'

Nerves were high. The actors grabbed each other excitedly.
Shirley hovered around the edges looking for a friendly cluster.
She found Gail clinging to the back of the leading man, and
leant against her, patting her on the arms. Nigel seized her from
behind.

'Shirley, you're costume assistant, right? Thought so, I need
you.'

She followed him up the steps to the back of the lecture
theatre. Nigel threw himself into row Q and howled.

'I'm in crisis.'

Shirley was alarmed. She looked back to Gail, who was kissing
the stage manager.

'Why?'

'Oh, Shirley! Shirls!'

Shirley shifted from foot to foot.

'I have lost the very centre of the performance, the whole
rhythm and meaning that we've been struggling for.'

Shirley's face was blank. He spelt it out for her.

'The drum, Shirley. We are *sans* drum.' He put his arm
around her. 'Shirley, think of our company, of the hours of

improvisation behind this production. How do we hold **all** that energy together?'

Shirley shrugged apologetically.

'The beat, that's how! I ask you, Shirley, what is the wailing scene without the drum?'

He let go of her and held his head in his hands.

'I've just had Stacey's mother on the phone and it seems that Stacey has spent the day slicing both of her wrists.'

'Oh, poor Stacey! Do you want me to organise the card?'

'No, Shirley, I want you to bang the sodding drum.'

Shirley's eyes were wide with fear. 'But I'm supposed to help Gail with the hangers.'

'Not any more. Now you remember what Stacey did. Up front, centre stage, you hit the drum every five seconds. Fabulous. Here's Crystal with it now.'

Crystal gave the drum to Shirley. She took it dumbly, her mind still snagging on the words 'centre stage'.

'When I hear that drum tonight, it's got to be the rhythm of life itself that I'm hearing. It's the beat of my heart, it's the pounding of my pulse, and underneath all that life, Shirley, it's the relentless and terrifying march of death.' He paused. 'Do you think you can give me that, Shirley? Let's try it **now**.'

Shirley hit the drum. Bang.

'No, Shirley, I want passion, think life.'

Shirley imagined Greg holding her in his arms. **Bang**.

'That's it. Now death.'

She thought about her Shakespeare exam.

'Great, now bring those two thoughts together. Give me the agony of that eternal struggle between life and death, between Eros and Thanatos.'

Shirley braced herself. She considered Greg reading *Henry V.* Then she got it.

Bang.

'Wonderful! Again.'

Bang.

'That's it, Shirley. I hear the torment. Keep thinking those thoughts.'

Shirley gave an involuntary shudder at the lingering image of her parents having sex.

'And remember, every five seconds.'

Nigel took the drum. 'I'll put this on stage, you're on front of house.' He raised his voice. 'Okay, people, places please. Off you go, front-of-house people, and remember, character, character, character! We're all actors now.'

Gail grabbed Shirley and they followed Rebecca, who was doing make-up, out to the foyer. It was their job to escort the audience into the auditorium. It was all part of the play. They were dressed in nurse's uniforms and had to treat everyone as if they were insane and being incarcerated in Bedlam. They were under Nigel's strict instructions not to drop out of character or explain anything to anyone. Their cue was the music, Fun Boy Three singing 'The Lunatics Have Taken Over the Asylum'. It worked brilliantly in rehearsals.

Shirley pushed into the crowd, silently practising her lines: 'Get in there! Lunatics like you should be locked up.'

She tried them out on a group of parents sipping orange juice from plastic cups. Their reaction was unexpectedly hostile. One of the women even threatened to become quite violent. Shirley skulked off, apologising. She saw her mother at the door, peering across the foyer, and fought her way through.

'Oh Shirley, don't you look fabulous! I'm sorry we're late.' She kissed her on each cheek, leaving bright fuschia lip prints. 'That's just how you looked on your fourth birthday. Where do the years go?'

Shirley rubbed her face. 'Stop it, Mum! I'm in character. I'm not supposed to know you.'

Gordon was close behind.

'Has your mother told you about the journey we had to get here? The last hour's been terrible, the M25 was totally chock-a-block. I've told your mother, I'm joining Charlie Cruikshank's campaign to Mount More Motorways.'

Shirley thought about banging the drum.

'Dad, I don't want to talk about road building, you know I

don't believe in that now. And anyway, I'm in character. I'm supposed to take the audience inside like they're all lunatics.'

'You're doing what?'

'That's my part! I say "Lunatics like you should be locked up"'.

'You say what?' He looked around at the assembled parents and lecturing staff. 'You can't talk to decent people like that. It's not as if they're students.'

'It's the play, Dad. It's all set in a lunatic asylum. It's about going mad. We improvised it all ourselves in rehearsals.'

'I thought you were doing a proper play.'

'It is a proper play!' Shirley kicked the ground. 'I might have known you wouldn't understand.'

Her mother took her by the arm. 'Don't listen to your father. He wouldn't know art if it whacked him round the head with a golf club. Now Shirley, say your line to me.'

Shirley herded her mother into Lecture Theatre A while her father ambled behind. She sat them on separate benches. Then, in character, she told several rows to sit up properly and stop talking. Her mother clapped loudly and leant over to the woman next to her.

'That's my daughter. She had an outfit just like that on her fourth birthday. I could weep just looking at her.'

The lights dimmed slightly and Shirley hurried to her drum. It went suddenly quiet and Gail's voice rang out from the back.

'And bloody stay quiet, scum!' She was thoroughly absorbed into character.

There was a sharp intake of breath. Instead of the expected blackout, the audience was blinded by a whiteout. Nigel saw it as defamiliarising the experience of theatre. Sixteen fixed lights were aimed directly into the faces of the audience, and Iain and his friend Malc were picking out individuals with the spots. Shirley saw her parents squint painfully into the glare. Then at Nigel's signal, the entire cast screamed for one minute and twenty-three seconds. Several members of the audience leapt up at the opening shrieks, but after the first minute they were all fairly subdued. Nigel gave them the thumbs up from the wings.

He had planned random screaming and whiteouts throughout the entire performance to symbolise how insanity illuminates the scourge of conformity and declares the banality of bourgeois reality. Very few parents realised these deeper levels of meaning. The auditorium was noticeably barer after the interval.

When the cast took their final bow Pearl was alone in giving them a standing ovation. She raced around to Lecture Theatre B and called out for Shirley.

'You're not allowed in here, Mum.'

'Oh, it's only me.' She raised her voice. 'I just popped in to say that I thought you were all wonderful.' She turned back to Shirley. 'I only wish I'd brought Lucasta with me, instead of your bloody father.'

Nigel rushed up to meet her. 'Here's my favourite mum!' They shook hands and Shirley did the introductions. 'So you liked it, Mrs Gates?'

'It was very artistic, very different.'

'Too different for most of them out there.'

'Listen, Nigel, you don't want to bother about those people like Shirley's father who walked out. Old miseries, the lot of them. They need a bit of shaking up.'

'Magnifico, Mrs Gates!' He threw his arms around Pearl and held her by the shoulders. 'Those are exactly the sentiments I was trying to convey in the production. A resistance to the bland righteousness of the moral majority who reject the multiplicity of postmodern potentialities with fantasised nostalgia.'

Pearl frowned in confusion at her daughter, but Shirley didn't understand him either.

'People like Gordon don't like anything new, that's all.'

'Because it challenges their hegemony.'

'Well, I don't know about that, Nigel. He just likes things his own way.'

'But you, Mrs Gates, you have saved us from the Philistines! If our little drama spoke to you, and you alone, in the entire auditorium, then I have succeeded!'

He held both of Pearl's hands.

'Mrs Gates, Pearl, will you promise me something? Don't waste this moment. When art speaks to you, listen to it!'

Shirley looked from Nigel to her mother and felt uneasy. A strange light was shining in her mother's eyes.

'Wait here, Shirley. I need to make a phone call.'

When they got to the car, it was locked and the sleet was beginning to turn to snow. Gordon had left them instructions and a set of directions in a small plastic bag tied to the wind-screen wipers. Twenty minutes later, they found him reading the *Telegraph* at the back of Clinkers wine bar. He folded it on his lap when he saw them.

'Ah, you've finished all that dreadful nonsense, have you, Shirley?'

Shirley looked to her mother to defend her, but she didn't. Pearl had other things on her mind. She gave Shirley her purse and sent her to get the drinks.

'And take your time. There's something I need to tell your father.'

When Shirley came back with two white wines and a whisky, her dad had his head in his hands. He was crying. Shirley looked from him to her mum, appalled. Her mum was horribly calm.

'Sit down, Shirley. I've got something to tell you.'

Pearl took the whisky and drank it straight.

'I've made a decision about my future. A hard decision, but a necessary one. For me. This will be difficult for you to under-stand right now, Shirley, but I'm sure you will in time.'

She paused. Shirley felt scared.

'I'm divorcing your father. I have my reasons. Your father knows very well what they are, but I won't trouble you, love, with the sordid details. I'm moving on, Shirley, and I would like you to move with me. I have just phoned Cass, and from tomorrow I will start work at the Cosmic Café. I'll be living there too. I'll collect my things from home next week. I hope you can be happy for me.'

Gordon started to whimper into his Chardonnay. Shirley was furious.

'I don't believe you! What about Dad? What about me?'

'I'm sorry you're upset, Shirley, but frankly you are both quite capable of looking after yourselves. I'll still be here for you, of course. Even more so now I'm in London. But I'm also going to look after myself. You'll get used to it.'

Shirley shook her head in disbelief. 'God, you're so selfish! Don't you care what this is doing to Dad?'

Pearl didn't answer. Gordon was still sobbing.

'And what if I don't want you in London? Why do you have come here anyway?'

'Because I want to be near you, Shirley, and also because I've found the café.'

'And what about Dad? I'll just give up everything and look after him in Frinley, shall I?'

'Don't be silly, Shirley. You will understand one day, I promise.'

Shirley refused to look at her. 'Just go then, if you're going!'

Pearl got up. 'Right! I'm sure I can find my own way to Balham.'

They watched her go in silence.

Chapter 24

A New Member

It was Monday morning and the Cosmic Café wasn't yet open. The debris from the night before's Stir-fry Special still littered the floor. Dee switched on the urn and filled a kettle for the collective meeting.

'So do you know what this is all about then, Jaz?'

Jasbinder was spinning around on one of the stools near the counter. She revolved slowly until she was face to face with Dee. 'I just got a message. Cass spoke to Kumar. She said it was good news though.' She pushed off the counter with her feet, turning her head as the stool rotated around. 'I thought you and Buzz would know more. Didn't Cass come in last night?'

'Nope! Just rang up and rang off. Buzz got it.'

'So what did she say to him?'

'Same as you. I wish she wouldn't play these silly bloody games.'

Jaz spun the other way. 'Perhaps she's won the lottery.'

'My arse!' Dee spooned coffee into two of the cups. 'I suppose you want one of your herbal concoctions?' She picked up the pot ready for Jaz's instructions.

'I've invented a new one.' Jaz pointed to the shelf above Dee's head. Large glass jars held different coloured flowers, leaves and powders. It was a sweet shop for the health-conscious. 'Two spoons of hibiscus, two spoons of elderflower, one of peppermint and a pinch of ginger. I was going to make some up for the café, but I don't know if it's worth it now. Anyway, I couldn't decide what to call it.'

'Well, I call it a load of messing about for smelly hot water. How's that?'

'Not very good, Dee. I was thinking of this really cool thing of putting all the first letters together, you know like Pheg or Ghep, but I think I'll probably go for "Jaz's Mix" again. This'll be Jaz's Mix no.11.'

Dee put the different jars back on the shelf. 'How about, "Now! That's What I Call Tea" . . .'

Jaz grinned and stirred the pot. 'Do you think Buzz might know something?'

They could both hear him coming down the stairs from the kitchens, coughing up enough tar to surface a road.

Dee made a face. 'I doubt it somehow.'

Buzz came in through the back, rolling a cigarette. 'Is that coffee made, Dee?' He sat down with his legs stretched out.

'Coming right up.'

'No sign of Cass, then?' He flicked a dead match onto the floor and kicked his feet up on to the table. Dee took the coffees over and pulled up a chair. Jaz followed.

'So do you know what this is all about, Buzz?'

He nodded, inhaling deeply on a skinny roll-up. 'I'm afraid that I do. I hope I'm wrong, but I fear I'm right.'

Dee rolled her eyes at Jasbinder. Buzz was in his fire-and-brimstone mood.

'It's my opinion that Cass has found us someone with money.'

'Well, let's fucking hope so!' Dee sipped at her coffee.

'Someone who will buy their way on to the collective.'

'It just gets better!'

Buzz stamped on his cigarette. 'We don't want that kind of interference. That's not what this café's about.'

Dee laughed. 'Buzz, we're up shit creek, don't dis the paddle.'

The café door opened, knocking the wind chimes on the ceiling. Cass came in, beaming, stamping the slush off her boots.

'I've got someone here that I want you to meet.'

She held her hand out to Pearl, who was still hovering in the street behind her. 'This is Pearl. She's the good news I told you about on the phone.'

Pearl smiled nervously as she came through the door.

'And listen to this. Not only does Pearl want to become a member of the co-op, she also wants to invest £10,000 in the business and rent the empty rooms upstairs.'

Jaz and Dee clapped and cheered. Cass danced across the café to join them.

Pearl was left by herself at the counter, feeling uncomfortably like a winning lottery ticket. She watched them all celebrating and wrestled with the sickening feeling that Gordon might have been right all along. Maybe she was exactly what he said she was, a stupid housewife being conned by a group of scheming weirdos. Sitting at the table in front of her, chatting and laughing, were a pink-haired lesbian, a tiny Indian girl a bit older than Shirley, and a fat African woman about the same age as Cass. Next to them, a skin-headed hooligan in his early forties stared, unsmiling, at the floor. What had she been thinking of?

She turned away from the collective to look around at the café itself. Above the counter brightly painted menus offered nachos, biriani and tabouli; noticeboards were crammed with posters; and stars shone on the purple ceiling. The whole place was a mess, the floor was filthy, the counter littered with dirty glasses and ashtrays, and the staff in need of a good wash. But it was just what she needed. A second chance away from Gordon and the dowagers of Frinley. They could say what they liked at the golf club. This place had potential. It was alive with possibilities. And she was going to make it work.

She adjusted the front of her dress and walked to the table. Cass smiled and introduced her to Jasbinder and Dee. They shook hands politely. Then she introduced Buzz. He ignored Pearl's outstretched hand and simply looked her up and down, his jaw twitching. Pearl tried a different approach.

'Do you know, I've always wondered what hair like yours feels like, do you mind if I . . .?' She patted him on the head. 'Oh, it's all fluffy. How funny!'

Dee slapped the table and howled. Buzz stared at Pearl with undisguised horror. She smiled her best dinner party smile and sat down.

'I was only joking with you, dear.'

He stared at her, at her expensively set hair, her department store dress, and her gold jewellery. She was the living embodiment of pampered stupidity. A fully paid-up member of the petty bourgeoisie. He sneered into his tobacco and spat on the floor between them. Pearl inched her chair away from the stain.

'I don't think you should spit in here, do you? It's no wonder you've got trouble with the hygiene people.'

Buzz grimaced, licking the paper and rolling it around his tobacco.

'And if you've got a bad throat, that's the first thing you should give up.'

He looked menacingly at Cass, but she was chatting with the others and didn't notice his hostility. 'Of course, we as the collective have to approve Pearl as a new member, but if we can agree to that, as if we wouldn't,' she laughed excitedly, 'it looks like the café is saved!'

Jasbinder smiled nervously at Pearl, glancing at Buzz. Dee raised her hand as if voting. 'She's approved.'

Cass cheered. 'The Cosmic Café lives on! We should all drink to our new member. Buzz, will you get one of those bottles of Chardonnay from the fridge?'

Buzz stayed where he was. 'We haven't had a formal vote.'

Dee groaned loudly, but Cass shut her up.

'All right, Buzz. We'll do it properly. All those in favour of accepting Pearl as a member of the collective say aye.'

Only Buzz stayed silent. Cass began to look worried.

'Buzz?'

He fixed Pearl with his good eye. 'I don't want her.'

There was an edgy silence. Cass looked to Pearl, then back to Buzz.

'What?'

'She's not right for the café.'

'What do you mean, not right for the café? This is our chance to save the bloody café.'

He sneered at her. 'You mean this is our chance to join the oppressors.'

Cass appealed to him. 'Oh come on, Buzz, Pearl's hardly an agent of the state.'

He stood up. 'She's buying you! And you all jump at the chance to sell out.'

Dee shook her head. 'Nobody's buying anyone, you stupid Trotsky. She's joining as a member of the collective, an equal member.'

'Yeah!' Buzz spoke directly to Pearl. 'And some members are more equal than others, isn't that right?'

Pearl flushed. She wasn't used to being the focus of ideological debate. And her idea of unequal members was more Jackie Collins than George Orwell.

'I do have experience, you know.'

'Right!' Cass gestured for them all to sit down. 'If you've got a problem, Buzz, then we'll do this by the rules. You can't reject someone put forward by another member without giving them an interview. Pearl, is it all right if we ask you a few questions, just to get this sorted out?'

Pearl nodded, folding her hands in her lap. 'Fire away!'

'Okay, first I'll go over some of things I've already told you about the café, just for the record, and then you can tell us something about yourself and why you want to join the collective. Jaz, will you get some paper for minutes?' She paused, waiting for Jaz to get back. 'Right! I'm the chair of the collective, but we all share the work and we all share the profits, which normally gives us enough to live on. And as I said to you last night, we've got twelve years left on the leasehold for this place, and the co-op owns everything in it collectively. If we ever cease trading, then the creditors get first pick of the bones before the collective splits the rest. Okay, everyone?'

They all nodded.

'Now, let's start this interview by you telling us about your relevant experience. For instance, have you worked in kitchens or at tables before? Have you got any bookkeeping qualifications? Anything you think that might be useful to the café?'

Pearl coughed and sat up very straight. 'Well, Cass, as you know, I'm recently separated from my husband Gordon after twenty-five years of marriage, and frankly I think those years have given me all the experience I'll ever need.'

They all waited for her to go on, but she sat back with her arms folded as if that said it all. Buzz was the first to speak. 'This is a radical co-op not the fucking WI! Marriage is a religio-imperialist plot to keep women and the workers down. It's not work experience.'

Pearl pursed her lips. 'Have you ever been married?'

'I refuse to engage in the socio–legitimation practices of the nation state.'

'I see, well, I'll take that as a no. It seems to me, young man, that you're jumping the gun a bit with me. If you'd spent twenty-five years with Gordon, believe me, you'd call it an experience. Now look!' She spread her hands across the table. 'What do you do when you run a café? You cook things, you serve them up, you clean them up, and you work out the costs. Now I've been doing that for twenty-five years and I've been doing it well. I'm a dab hand at making the housekeeping stretch. How else do you think I saved that £10,000? And I've not just been cooking for Gordon and Shirley, oh no. I've hosted more dinner parties than you can shake a stick at. I'd like to see you make a Beef Bourguignonne for sixty-five and keep a smile on your face.'

She sat back. Cass looked between her and Buzz.

'Well, Buzz, I think that gives us something to go on. I mean, Pearl obviously knows what she's doing in the kitchen.'

'Cooking meat.'

Pearl rose to the challenge. 'I can do some pretty mean things with a vegetable when roused.'

He grunted. Cass intervened. 'I've explained to Pearl that we have a strict vegetarian policy here. That's not going to change.'

'Anyway, Buzz.' Pearl handled his name as if it was an exotic insect. 'If I've been held back by the Lego–Socio–Imperials while I was married to Gordon, shouldn't you be helping me to get out and do something like this instead?'

Dee laughed. 'She's got you there, Buzz.'

'I mean, if you don't think people's ideas can change, why do you do all those politics?'

Buzz pushed out his chin. 'I'm working for the revolution when the workers will smash the bourgeoisie and control the means of production.'

'Right!' Pearl had the same tone she used on Shirley 'Well, until the likes of me are all up against the wall, how about keeping this café going, so your friends here don't end up without a job? Think about that, will you? What's Cass going to do if this place closes when she's got a baby on the way and no job?'

There was an uncomfortable silence. Jasbinder curled up in her chair. Cass answered her.

'That's not really fair pressure, Pearl. Buzz has the right to make a political stand.'

'Stand? Rights be buggered! This is the real world I'm talking about. And if you don't get my money, that's it, the café's finished. Never mind all this politics malarky, if he stops me joining today it all goes down the swanny.'

Buzz was twitching furiously.

'Well, are you going to let everyone down or not?'

Jaz was hugging her knees, staring at the floor. She looked askance at Pearl. No one had ever spoken to Buzz like that before. Not even Dee.

Buzz stood up slowly and spoke directly to Cass. 'I would like a minuted record that I have only conceded to this woman joining the collective because the agents of oppression have forced us to our knees. I want it recorded that I warned you all about selling out and that I have grave fears for the political integrity of future café policy.'

Pearl looked at Cass. 'Is that a yes, then?'

Cass nodded. Dee raised her hands to the ceiling. 'Amen and hallelujah. Now can we please have that drink?'

Chapter 25

Opening Night

'Oh my God, Cass, you're wearing a dress!' Andy reeled back in mock horror. 'And it's pink.'

Cass gave a twirl. 'Do you like it?'

'Of course I do, sweetie.' Andy kissed her on each cheek. 'You look fabulous. Here. Flowers for the new-look café.'

'Andy, that's so sweet.' Cass found a teapot behind the counter and filled it with water. 'When we open,' she looked at her watch, 'in ten minutes, we'll be the New Cosmic Café. But don't say anything to Buzz, he'll give you a lecture on Blairism and New Labour.'

'Darling, I *never* say anything to Buzz. Anyway, look at this place!' He wandered around the tables. 'You have been busy bees. I never thought this old café would scrub up so well.'

'Never mind scrub, we've practically gutted it.'

'And here was me thinking you'd done a quick flick with the duster.'

Cass sneered at him. 'Just wait 'til you see the kitchen, you won't recognise it. It's fabulous! And look at our shiny new counter.' She leant over it provocatively. 'It's so sexy, I love it.'

'Yes, well remember your Food Hygiene Course. Rule no. 4: "Never get too sticky near food preparation surfaces."'

She threw a daffodil at him.

'I see you kept your vile colour scheme.'

'Hey, I like orange and purple. It's the only thing in the whole damn place that hasn't changed, and even that's been "spruced up".' She came out from behind the counter with a bottle of red wine. 'You know, I am so sick of hearing that phrase. I've told Pearl that if she says it one more time I'm going to let Buzz shoot her.'

Andy laughed. 'They're still not seeing eye to eye, then?'

'There's been a bit of an upset with the new dumb waiter.' Cass smiled wickedly and glanced up, checking the back door to the kitchens was closed. 'Pearl's made such a thing about having this bloody dumb waiter, and it's been a total aggravation from start to finish. Buzz hates it. Anyway, we finally got it working yesterday, and Pearl gathered us around the bottom for the official opening. Andy, she was practically cutting a ribbon!' She grinned. 'She'd left Buzz in the kitchen with this bowl of chilli that we were supposed to be having for lunch, ready to send it down. So we're all waiting, and nothing happens. Pearl keeps opening the doors. Nothing. So she beeps up to him on the intercom and has a bit of a go about him being so slow.' Cass rolled her eyes. 'That's one of their many themes over the last two weeks. Anyway, then there's this rumbling from above. So Pearl rushes back to position, opens the door and whoosh, there's the chilli hurtling down at about ninety miles per hour.' They started to laugh. 'Of course it hits the bottom and splat, chilli flying everywhere. Pearl got completely covered. Even her hairdo was full of kidney beans.'

There was a wailing from behind the counter. Andy looked alarmed. Cass got up, still giggling.

'Don't worry, that's the intercom, neat hey?'

She pressed the button. 'Yes?'

A fuzzy voice blared out. 'Is Shirley here yet, Cass?'

'No, Pearl, and stop worrying. I'll let you know when she gets here.' She released the button.

Andy had his hands over his ears. 'Don't you think you should turn that thing down?'

'No, it needs to be loud for when it's busy. Trust me.'

She opened the wine as the back door swung open. Pearl was standing there with two trays.

'It's only us.'

Buzz slouched behind her.

'We've brought down the nibbles. They always get a party off to a good start.' She looked around. 'Aren't the band here yet?'

'They'll be here!' Buzz slammed down his trays. 'Gizmo's a mate.'

Andy leant over to see what they'd brought down. 'Canapés, how marvellous. What have we got? Vol-au-vents, cheese straws, oh, and my personal favourite, veggie sausage on a stick.' He popped one into his mouth. 'Fabulous!'

Pearl smiled at him. 'What did I tell you, Buzz. People always love a nibble, even vegetarians. Anyway, I'm off. I've left Dee struggling with my lasagne sauce upstairs.'

'You should have sent the vol-au-vents down in that, Pearl.' Andy pointed to the dumb waiter. 'Saved yourself the trip.'

Pearl's face flushed. 'Unfortunately, it goes rather fast, dear. Especially if people aren't careful with it.' She stared at Buzz. 'But I'm sure we'll get the hang of it tonight. Anyway, must dash.'

Cass picked up a tray as Pearl disappeared through the back door. 'Buzz, do you think we should put some of these things on each table or just put the trays on the counter?'

He shrugged. 'You sort it, Cass, Gizmo's here.'

Outside, four dreadlocked comrades of various ethnicity were unloading a van. Buzz opened the door.

'Sorry we're late, mate. Trouble getting an amp.' Gizmo waved at Cass.

Buzz nodded. 'It happens.'

'So where do you want us?' He looked across the laid tables and noticed the platform at the back. 'Wow, a stage. Serious! Where shall we hang the banner?'

The Tooting Hottentots had played several times at the café, always to a mixed reception. It was a big concession to Buzz that they were playing the opening night. Cass brought over four bottles of lager. 'Remember guys, nice and quiet tonight. We want people eating not vomiting. Keep all the heavy stuff until after eleven.'

'No worries, sister. We're unplugged tonight, no amp.'

Cass laughed. 'But your entire sound is feedback. What are you going to do?'

'Hey, unkind sister! We've got reggae, klezmer and folk roots here. We're going back to the sounds of the people.'

'Right!' Cass raised her eyebrows. 'Sounds of the people. Perfect.'

More wailing from the counter. It was Dee on the intercom.

'Lasagne's coming down.'

'Okay, keep it slow, Dee.'

'Yeah, and stand well back.' They both laughed and the intercom grated loudly as Cass let go of the button.

Gizmo shouted over. 'Hey, sister, great sound! Can we use that later?'

By half-past eight, every table was full. Pearl beamed as she trotted around offering sweetcorn vol-au-vents to anyone who would take one. Cass and Dee were serving behind the counter. Cass buzzed up to the kitchen.

'Jaz, tell Buzz we need more lasagne down here, one of each bowl of salad, and I've got eight orders for nachos.'

She turned back to Dee.

'This is fantastic. We've never had such a good night.'

'Yeah, I'm just waiting for Gizmo and his mates to start clearing them out.'

'Don't say that, Dee. Anyway, I think even they might be quite good tonight.' Cass cleared the empty bowls of salad.

'What, Citizen Smith and the Tooting Popular Front? You are joking!'

Cass leant towards her. 'I'll let you into a secret. They've lost their amp.' They both laughed and Cass took the empty bowls to the dumbwaiter. Pearl grabbed her by the pulley.

'Have you seen Shirley yet?'

'Sorry, Pearl, there's no sign of her.'

Pearl sighed. 'I don't think she's coming. I really thought she would. Just tonight. For me.'

'Well, it's not too late. I'm still waiting for Anna.' Cass put her hand on Pearl's arm. 'I'm sure Shirley will come soon.'

Pearl gave her a brave smile. 'Well, not to worry. Here's Anna with Ruby now. She looks a bit peaky, Cass. Is she all right?'

Cass hurried over to the door. 'Hi, Ruby. Anna, I was getting worried. Are you all right? You look pale.'

Anna kissed her. 'I'm fine, just a bit tired. The café looks fantastic, Cass. There are so many people here.'

'Come on, I saved you a table. It's the one furthest away from the band.' Cass smiled as she guided Anna to her chair. 'I'm so glad you're here, my love. Andy's been here hours. I think he's pissed already.'

'I heard that!' Andy kissed Anna as she sat down. 'Honestly, you can't get the staff.'

Anna smiled. 'It's Ruby's fault we're late. She's been through her entire wardrobe twice.'

Ruby picked up a cheese straw. 'Well, it's all right for you, Anna. Who expects glamour when you've a figure like the Dome on legs?'

Anna laughed. 'Watch it, cheeky. Anyway, I know what you're up to.'

Ruby feigned innocence. 'Up to?'

'Yes, hussy breath. He's sitting over there.' Anna pointed to Johnnie, who was on the other side of the café.

'I don't know who you mean.'

'I'll call him over to remind you, shall I?' Ruby hissed threats as Anna waved and gestured to Johnnie. Anna smiled back at her. 'He's coming over. And so is that woman from his house.'

'Hi, Anna, Andy.' Johnnie stood awkwardly by the table while Annabel draped herself all over him. 'Hello, Ruby. How are you?'

'Fine.' Ruby faked serenity. 'I see you're keeping on top of things.' She arched an eyebrow in Annabel's direction.

'Not really.' He held her stare. 'It's been a long, cold month.'

Annabel cooed loudly over his shoulder. 'Johnnie, aren't you going to introduce your new girlfriend?'

Ruby dismissed her. 'We know who you are. We live across the road, remember?'

She simpered back. 'How could I forget?'

Johnnie looked flustered. 'Yeah, Annabel's a housemate.'

Annabel laughed. 'Housemate? I think you mean bedmate, Johnnie. Or are you sleeping with Jenni and Shirley too?' She smiled smugly at Ruby, slipping her manicured hand into Johnnie's front pocket. Ruby stared nonchalantly back. 'Such a homely harem you've got, Johnnie.' She paused to let the insult sink in.

Andy stood up. 'Quick, Johnnie, someone's after your table. You better get back there.'

Johnnie hesitated, trying to catch Ruby's eye, but she refused to look at him. He nodded to Andy before leaving their table. 'Thanks, mate. Perhaps I'll see you around then, Ruby.'

'Perhaps.'

Annabel lingered behind, desperate for the last word. 'You oldies have a good time now, before you forget how.'

Anna was opened-mouthed. 'God, that woman's a bitch. What's Johnnie doing with her?'

Ruby pulled out her Colt 45 lighter. 'Fucking her. Or did I hear wrong?' She lit her cigarette.

'Ruby, I'm so sorry. I didn't mean to upset you. I thought I was doing you a favour.'

'Who's upset? I'm enjoying myself. Right, let's eat, drink and be merry.'

They picked up the menus.

Cass put her hands on Anna's shoulders. 'What did you think of the food, then?'

Andy gave her his empty plate. 'Sweetie, that spinach lasagne was superb. Tony would be green if he tasted it.'

Cass half smiled. 'Shame he couldn't make it tonight.'

Andy looked embarrassed. 'He's working.'

She nodded. 'I see. Anyway, Anna, you've hardly touched yours, didn't you like it?'

Anna looked up at her. 'No, it was lovely, honest. I'm just not very hungry. Must be the baby pressing on my stomach.'

'Are you sure you're okay?' Cass looked at the others. 'Has she been all right?'

Anna slapped her hand. 'Yes, she's been fine. If you want to talk about me at least wait until I'm in the loo.'

Cass helped her up. 'Just take it easy.'

'I will.' She rested on her arm. 'To be honest, honey, I do feel a bit weak. I might go home soon, do you mind?'

'No, of course not. Go to bed, get some sleep.'

'I don't want to ruin your night.'

'Don't be silly. Go!'

Anna smiled. 'I'll just nip to the loo first.' Cass watched her walk slowly to the back of the café before clearing the next table.

Buzz grabbed her arm. 'Hey, Cass, I've swapped places with Dee 'cause Gizmo and the lads are starting now. It's gone ten.'

Cass faked a smile. 'Great. In that case I think I'll join her in the kitchen.'

Buzz jerked after her to the stage. 'I'll announce them then, shall I?' He jumped on the platform at the back of the café. 'Brothers and sisters, comrades. Welcome back to the Cosmic. There's been some changes here, but we're still a radical place for radical people and we've got Tooting's most radical band playing for us tonight. The Tooting Hottentots!'

Gizmo took centre stage and began stamping out the beat of their signature tune, 'Roll on Revolution.' Behind him the others were banging on the walls and floor with sticks, chanting 'revolution, revolution, revolution'. Gizmo urged the diners to clap the rhythm. Ruby stood up, stamping her feet and chanting.

Andy stared at her. 'What the hell are you doing, woman? Have you become a Trot?'

She grinned at him. 'I'm having "a good time", and I'd be very grateful if you'd join me.'

Andy looked at Gizmo and made a face. 'Oh, all right, since

it's you!' He got up and minced over to Ruby chanting, 'revolution, revolution, shevolution, shaving lotion'.

Within minutes the entire café was on its feet, stamping and chanting. The sounds of revolution, unintentionally syncopated, filled the room. No one saw Anna as she staggered back from the loo. She gripped the piano and looked for Cass, but she couldn't see above the noise and the blur of faces. Her legs were weak and she sank down quietly on to the floor beside the stage. The aching in her belly was getting worse and her head throbbed. She closed her eyes to shut out the pain.

Mutley, Gizmo's brother, was the first to notice her. He knelt over her with his drumsticks.

'Hey, sister. Are you all right?'

Anna opened her eyes and tried to focus on his unfamiliar face. She strained to speak, to say Cass's name, but it was no more than a whisper and he didn't understand. She gave up, closing her eyes against the effort. He caught her in his arms as she slumped sideways, grazing her face on the rough edge of the stage. He pulled her on to the platform and shouted to his brother.

'Gizmo! Stop, man! Get an ambulance!'

Ruby and Andy were still chanting to each other.

'Raving notion!'

'Clever potion!'

'Have a motion!'

Gizmo shouted from the stage, struggling to be heard above the noise. 'There's a pregnant woman collapsed here. Does anyone know her?'

'Leather fusion'

'Never douche hon.'

'I love you son.'

The stamping and banging suddenly stopped. Someone was shouting at everyone to sit down and be quiet, but more and more people were gathering at the back of the café, crowding noisily around the stage. Then Ruby heard Johnnie calling her.

'Ruby. It's Anna, Ruby. She's collapsed.'

Ruby grabbed Andy's arm and they both rushed to the stage.

'Anna, oh my God!' Andy reached her first, pushing the crowd out of the way. He stroked her face while Gizmo and Mutley stood over him, gawping.

'It's Andy. Can you hear me, sweetie?'

Ruby charged through. 'Is she all right, Andy?'

'She's unconscious.'

'Oh fuck!' She turned on Gizmo. 'Don't just stand there, you moron, call a fucking ambulance.'

Andy stood up and yelled across the chaos. 'Someone call an ambulance and get Cass!' The noise of speculation was rising. 'And get all these people out of here!' As he spoke Dee came back into the café to check on the Hottentots. She glanced at what was happening on the stage and immediately took charge.

Andy crouched back down. Ruby had covered Anna with her jacket. She had tears in her eyes. 'Andy, she's bleeding. I think she's losing the baby.'

Dee cleared the café within minutes. When she buzzed up to Cass in the kitchen, the last of the customers were leaving, throwing concerned glances back at the stage. The intercom grated as Dee flicked it off, and they could hear Cass running down the stairs. The back door burst open and she scrambled on to the stage, followed by Pearl and Jaz.

'Anna! Anna!' Cass knelt next to Anna's silent shape. She stared at her, her eyes wide with fear and then she charged at Ruby. 'What's happened to her? What's going on? What have you done to her?'

Dee grabbed her by the shoulder. 'Cass, this is no one's fault, don't look to blame. If Anna can hear, she needs you to be soft with her. The ambulance is on its way.'

Cass looked at her and nodded. She squeezed Ruby's hand in apology and lay down next to Anna. She spoke in a whisper. 'I'm here, Anna. I'm going to look after you. Everything will be all right now.'

The others climbed down from the platform, leaving Anna and Cass alone together on the stage. They waited in silence until the ambulance arrived twenty minutes later. The paramedics removed Ruby's jacket, now drenched in blood, and lifted

Anna on to the stretcher. Cass hugged Andy and Ruby as Anna was carried away.

'We'll follow you, darling. Andy and I'll get a taxi to the hospital. Anna and the baby will both be all right, you'll see.'

Cass followed the stretcher out of the café. Johnnie was standing on the pavement next to the ambulance. He held her arm as she clambered into the back. When it drove away, Pearl saw Shirley on the other side.

Chapter 26

After Hours

Shirley watched the ambulance from the other side of the street. It had sped past her as she was walking down Balham High Street, and she'd watched, horrified, as it had crossed the road and slowed to a halt outside the café. She hadn't meant to come to the café tonight. She was still furious with her mother. Her dad was a laughing stock in Frinley because of her selfishness. Pearl had made a fool of herself and her family. And Shirley hated her for it.

When the ambulance had passed her, Shirley was thinking about her mother. She was thinking about what she would say to her to punish her for what she'd done. Then she saw it pull over to the café and her heart leapt. She raced down the street to catch up, trying desperately to see who the paramedics were taking away. She could see Cass crying as she climbed in behind them. Johnnie was with her. Then the doors were closed and the sirens sounded. The flashing lights on the roof glared blue against the falling snow as the ambulance turned around in the road and accelerated past her. Shirley was left panting on the edge of the pavement, watching it speed away from her, a scream of noise and lights disappearing into the falling snow.

She turned to face the café opposite. The sign above the door had been replaced. The New Cosmic Café shone amidst a background of neon stars that glimmered gently against purple-edged windows. The lights inside were bright, but the tables were empty. Then the door opened. Her mum was standing in the doorway, wearing a pale green robe decorated with thick gold brocade. Her hair was different. She was watching Shirley with tears in her eyes.

Shirley looked beyond her into the café. Johnnie was sitting at the end of a table, wiping his face and talking to someone she couldn't see. Pearl stretched her arms out, smiling sadly and Shirley walked slowly across the road towards her. Pearl squeezed her tightly in the doorway, whispering thank yous into her ear. Over her mum's shoulder, Shirley could see the others. Ruby was leaning over the table with her head in her hands sobbing, while next to her Andy stared silently into nothing. Johnnie watched them both from the end of the table. There were three others that she recognised as café workers making coffee and silently clearing tables. Nobody said a word.

Shirley pulled away from her mum.

'What's happened? Who was in the ambulance?'

Her mum wiped a tear from her cheek. 'It was Anna, Shirley. She collapsed a little while ago.'

Shirley stared at the others. 'But she's not . . . I mean, is she all right? Is the baby all right?'

Pearl shook her head. 'We don't know yet, Shirley.'

'But I . . .' She looked at Johnnie. 'Does Greg know?'

Ruby glanced up, her eyes red and bleary. She snorted at Shirley and her sad infatuation. 'No, young Shirley, he doesn't. But you're right, we should tell him. Greg would want to be here.'

Johnnie's chair scraped the floor as he got up. 'I'll ring him.'

Dee gave him the phone and went to lock the door.

'He's at home with Cori. She's got chickenpox.' Nobody was listening to Shirley. Ruby spoke over her.

'Johnnie, we'll need a taxi for the hospital.'

He nodded. 'I'll sort it.'

'I can't go.' They all looked at Andy. Ruby tried to hold his hand but he pulled it away. 'This is my fault. I did this to her.'

'No, you did not.' She grabbed his hand again. 'You gave her the chance to be a mother. She's always wanted a baby, and you were there for her.'

'Yes, well, forgive me, sweetie, but those cosy clichés do not help.' He stood up and walked to the back of the café.

The others stared after him. Ruby got up to follow, but Pearl called after him.

'You can't just abandon your family because you're scared.'

Shirley turned on her mother. 'How dare you say that to him when you've walked out on Dad! You know nothing about this.'

'Oh, but I do, Shirley. I know exactly what this feels like because I have felt it myself. All birth is scary, Andy, because no one comes into this world easily.' She turned back to Shirley. 'And it wasn't fear that made me walk out on your father, it was fear that stopped me.'

Pearl was walking over to Andy. She sat down in front of him and put her hands over his. For a terrible moment it seemed like he might hit her. Ruby hurried over, gesturing for Pearl to leave him, but she wouldn't.

'I bled like Anna, before I gave birth to Shirley.'

She paused, watching him, but he just stared at the table, teeth clenched.

'They told Gordon at the hospital to be prepared for the worst. That's what you're thinking isn't it? The worst.'

Ruby shook her head. 'This isn't helping, Pearl.'

'He left, you see. He couldn't take feeling that it was his fault. So he left me to die on my own.'

Ruby leapt up. 'For God's sake, Pearl! What are you trying to do? Anna is not going to fucking die. And we are going to that fucking hospital to be there for Cass!'

'That's what I'm saying. I didn't die, did I?'

'Shut up, both of you!' Andy hit his fists on the table. 'You don't even know what I'm talking about. How can you know what a shit I am? I'm not just scared for Anna and the baby.

I'm scared how I'll cope if Tony leaves me after this. I'm scared for myself!'

Pearl nodded. 'Of course you are. It's frightening being a parent, and you're about to become a father.'

'How can I be? Look at me! I'm a fucking mincing queen!'

Pearl was lost for words, but Andy wasn't interested in her anyway.

'My mother would be laughing at me tonight, oh God, yes, waving her finger at me with fucking glee. She told me I'd bring nothing but suffering into the world and she was right! God, I was arrogant to think I could be a father. I'm stained with sin, and I've killed Anna. My soul's rolled in the cesspit for so fucking long, she was right, I'm human pollution.'

'Bollocks!' Ruby was shouting. 'What do you think you've got? Sub-atomic sperm?'

Behind them somebody giggled. It was Shirley. She muffled her face in her hands. 'I'm sorry, I couldn't help it.'

But Ruby was smiling at her. She threw her head back and laughed. When Greg reached the café, he looked through the window, and saw her howling amid the dirty tables.

He was carrying Cori, wrapped in a blanket, in his arms. He stood for a while, watching Andy sitting with his heads in his hands. Johnnie had told him that Andy had refused to go to the hospital, but he was too shocked and upset about Anna to take it in. Watching him now, he could see the misery of Andy's misplaced guilt. Ruby had stopped laughing. She was standing on her own in the middle of the café and she looked terrible. She saw Greg outside and grabbed the keys from Dee to open the door. Greg smiled as he walked towards her, and she reached out to hug him and Cori, dragging them into the café. Shirley shut the door behind them.

'I can't believe it, Ruby. Why did this have to happen?'

She shrugged. 'Because life's a bitch?'

Greg shook his head. 'She'll be okay, you know. It's just a scare, I'm sure of it. How's Andy holding up?'

'Not good. He's off on one of his mother's Catholic guilt-trips. He's blaming himself for what's happened. He thinks he's poisoned Anna with his sins.'

Greg looked at Andy's ashen face. 'I'll talk to him. And you? How are you coping?'

'I'm through the weepy phase and on to derangement.' She crossed her eyes, flopping her head around. Greg smiled at her. 'No, I'm okay. I just want to get to the fucking hospital, but I can't go without Andy. Cass needs him. Make him understand that, Greg.'

Greg had introduced Andy to Anna and Cass five years ago, when he was working on Andy's flat. Cori was a baby then, and he was on his own. Andy had been good to him, recommended him to the landlords he worked for. He'd helped Greg get his handyman business off the ground.

Greg sat down next to Andy and Pearl got up, offering to take Cori. Greg refused and she wandered back to the counter where Dee was waiting for her, looking uncomfortable.

'Listen, Pearl, this is personal stuff. We should leave them to it. The three of us are off now.'

She gestured to Jaz and Buzz, who were both hovering by the counter. 'We were going to clear up and everything, but it can wait.'

Pearl nodded.

'If Cass needs us she'll call. Let me know if she does.'

Pearl held the door open, waiting to lock it behind them. Dee turned as she left. 'And Pearl, I think you should take your daughter upstairs.'

Shirley looked away as Pearl came over. Johnnie had brought Ruby back to the table and was rolling her a joint while she sat brooding over a cigarette. Pearl stood behind her. 'Shirley, why don't you come upstairs with me now?'

'No, thanks.'

'I need to talk to you.'

'Why? Don't you think you've said enough for one night?'

Ruby waved her hand. 'Leave it. This is not the night for a domestic.'

Pearl stared at Shirley, but she refused to look back. So Pearl brushed past Greg and Andy, placing a consoling hand on his head, and then went up the back stairs alone. Greg was stroking Cori's hair, talking quietly to Andy.

'I don't think I've ever been so scared as the night Cori was born.' He looked at her sleeping face, eyelashes fluttering with dreams. 'I knew Acorn would leave us as soon as she could. She didn't want any of it, me, the baby, the house. The whole idea of us bored her. She left me in no doubt about that.'

Johnnie came over with two bottles of beer and gave Greg the newly rolled spliff. Andy was lying across the table with his eyes closed. He didn't look up. Johnnie put his hand briefly on Greg's shoulder before going back to Ruby.

'When Acorn walked out on us, Anna kept me together. I don't know if I would still have Cori if it hadn't been for Anna. They looked after us both, her and Cass.'

He pushed the bottle into Andy's hand. 'I envy you.'

Andy opened his eyes and stared at Greg. 'You envy me? What's a sad old homo got on a virile stud like you?'

Greg laughed. 'Virile? It's been so long since I've scored, I wouldn't know what to do with it if I had the chance. Since Acorn left I've had a fucking lonely time of it. But you know that. You met some of those single mums from the playschool.'

Andy smiled. 'Oh yes, Beverley from West Bromich, I remember her well.'

Greg lowered his voice. 'Tell you something you don't know, though. When I was really low one time I asked Ruby for a bit of sympathy. It was a few years ago now. Don't mention that to Johnnie.' He glanced guiltily at the other table. 'But look at you. You've got the perfect set-up. This great friendship. These two wonderful women bringing up your baby. And you've still got your own life. You still get to have sex, for Christ's sake.'

Andy smirked. 'And that's not something to be sniffed at.'

Greg smiled. 'And there's something else. I envy you having this baby with Anna.' He offered Andy the spliff. 'That's another of my little secrets.'

Andy took it, leaning up on his elbow. 'Are you telling me you're in love with Anna?'

'Maybe.'

'Serious?'

'It was.'

'And have you told her?'

'No. There was never any point. I wasn't about to become a woman, even if I wasn't using my manhood. And besides, I really care about Cass too.' Andy passed him the spliff. 'You know Cass needs you at that hospital, don't you?' Greg took it, without catching his eye. 'And anyway, there's someone else now.'

Andy raised his eyebrows. 'You sly dog.'

'I'm not sure if it will happen, though. She's a bit young, you know, a student.'

Andy glanced across at Shirley. 'Am I right?'

Greg nodded.

'Well, this could be your lucky night.' Andy closed his eyes. 'What the fuck am I saying! Anna's in hospital and I'm saying crap like that.'

'It's not crap, Andy. It *will* be a lucky night because Anna's going to pull through and she's going to have her baby. She's a fighter, Andy. Think what she did at Luigi's.'

'Don't, Greg. I can't bear it.'

'She faced up to her fear, just like Cass is doing at the hospital. She's on her own, Andy. She needs you and Ruby to be there for her.' He got up. 'Listen, I need a piss. Hold Cori for me. You'll be holding your own baby soon.' He lifted her gently on to Andy's lap and walked to the back door.

He took his time in the gents and when he came back he could hear people leaving. He waited until it was quiet before opening the door. Only Shirley was waiting for him, with Cori yawning in her arms.

'Have they gone?'

'Yeah, Andy said to tell you thanks.'

'Right. And Johnnie went too, did he?'

'I think he wanted to be with Ruby.'

Greg nodded. 'So it's just the three of us. Shall I take her?' Cori had half woken up and was reaching towards her dad. 'I'll

just get her to sleep again. She wants me to sing her our song.'
He sat down with Cori on his lap, rocking her from side to side,
and began singing 'Perfect Day'.

He stroked her face as he whispered the final lines, watching
her snore softly in his arms, and then glanced at Shirley with
an embarrassed smile. 'Sorry about my terrible singing voice,
but it's the only thing that gets her to sleep. I think she's Lou
Reed's youngest fan.'

Shirley said nothing. There were tears in her eyes. She leant
forwards across the table, took his face in her hands and kissed
him.

Chapter 27

The Hospital

Cass sat alone on an orange vinyl chair. A small figure in a short pink dress in a bleak hospital corridor. Behind her a row of large permanently closed windows exposed a naked concrete quad. She watched herself in their reflection for a while, floating above the slabs outside in her orange chair. Everything was vague in that other world, even her fear. The strips of neon above her head hovered in the frozen sky like muzzled ghosts. Across the quad, windows stared back at her. Blind eyes, black and empty, offering nothing.

She turned back to the closed doors in front of her. Anna had been in surgery for an hour and Cass had seen nobody. A young doctor, rushing behind the paramedics, had promised to return, but no one had been back through those swing doors. She strained towards them. She wanted to storm through and demand answers. But the memory of Anna's face in the ambulance, masked and sunken, stopped her.

She sat on the edge of decision until her body ached. Then she jolted out of her chair and away from the doors, stumbling down the corridor. She was leaving. The night security guard looked out at her through toughened safety glass as she wandered across the yellow lines of the emergency bays. He smiled kindly, remembering her from the rush into the building, Anna unconscious on the trolley and Cass crying, running behind. He pointed to the coffee machine inside, as if that would help. Cass fled from his concern.

She walked with the snow in her face. She walked out of the hospital grounds and into the deserted streets. She walked without thinking. It was nearly midnight and the residential roads were empty and dark. Rows of closed brick boxes, scorning the insolence of streetlights. Cass wandered into the road and held her face up to the falling sky. If Anna was dying, she was dying with strangers. Cass reached for her, holding her arms out as if to grasp her spirit from the snow. But there was nothing. Her hands were empty. She was alone.

She slumped down in the road, tired and numb with cold. Helpless tears seeped over her face. She heard the car before she saw it. It was coming from behind her, slowly crawling up the road, making its way through the snow. She thought of just lying there, escaping the pain of the hospital. It was almost on top of her when she sprang to the kerb. She ran down the pavement away from the yelling driver and into the next street. She leant against a streetlight and sobbed. Across from her, a single light shone out from an upstairs window. A figure, a woman, was moving behind the blind, bending, disappearing, then again silhouetted. Cass watched her as she came to the window and pulled up the blind. She stood, looking out to the sky, with a baby in her arms, showing her child the snow. And Cass saw Anna. Anna as a mother. Anna with their baby. Alive. She wiped her face and stood transfixed. Then she was moving, running, racing back to the hospital.

Inside, the warmth shocked her. She was sodden and her dress clung to her cold skin. She stumbled through identical sets of doors and endless corridors, looking for Anna. Everywhere looked the same. And then she found Ruby, sitting alone on the orange chairs. She called out. Ruby rushed towards her with her arms out and mascara tears streaking her face. They stood together in the corridor. Ruby hugging Cass tightly while

Cass wept. At last Ruby led her back to the chairs, wrapping her in her coat.

Cass pulled the coat around her, speaking into its folds. 'Have you heard anything? Has a doctor come?'

Ruby stroked her head. 'No. Not since I've been here. They just said to wait here at reception. I'm so sorry we took so long, Cass, there were no taxis anywhere.'

'It's okay.' They were both quiet again, looking at the doors in front of them. 'Where's Andy? Is he here?'

'Yes. He's gone looking for you with Johnnie. They'll be back soon. Don't worry.'

Cass was shivering. 'Ruby, can I have a cup of coffee?'

'Of course. And I'll get you some chocolate. Will you be all right while I'm gone?'

Cass nodded.

'I won't be long.'

When the doctor came Cass was sitting in a too big coat and a wet dress, watching the drips roll slowly down her legs. He looked at her suspiciously.

'Are you the friend that came in with Anna Jones?'

She leapt up.

'Is she all right?'

'She's still in theatre.'

'But she's okay? It's going to be all right?'

'I'm afraid I can't tell you anything for certain at the moment. Your friend has suffered a placenta abruption.' He held his clipboard in front of him like a shield, tight against his chest. 'That means that the placenta has come away from the wall of the womb and Anna is haemorrhaging badly.' He sat down a few seats along and took a pen from his top pocket. 'I wanted to ask you about the father. Do you know how we can reach him?' He paused, looking at the chart on his lap. 'The surgeons are doing everything they can to save your friend and her baby, but in these circumstances, it's best to contact relatives quickly.'

'Cass is a relative.' Andy's voice sounded loud and wonderful behind Cass. 'She's Anna's partner.'

The doctor looked up. 'And you are?'

'Andrew Lewis.' He put his hand on Cass's shoulder. 'I'm the baby's father, and Cass is the baby's other mother.'

Confusion, then disapproval, flitted across the doctor's face. 'I see.' He put his pen back on to his clipboard. 'Well, Mr Lewis, if you would like to follow me into the relatives' room you'll all be more comfortable waiting there. One of the surgeons will come to see you as soon as they are out of theatre.'

Andy helped Cass up, putting his arm around her. 'Come on, Cass, it's all going to be okay. I just know it.'

'But what about Ruby?'

Cass felt someone touch her back. 'It's all right, darling. I'm right behind you.'

The relatives' room had brown weave chairs and a coffee table. Cass sat between Andy and Ruby under a Monet print and a poster for bereavement counselling. Johnnie gave them each a coffee. They sipped in silence. Cass held her empty cup between her palms.

'Why has this happened to us?'

'I don't know.' Andy put his arm around her.

'You don't think it's because we're gay?'

'Don't be silly, sweetie, of course not.' He looked over to Ruby, who smiled sadly back.

'But we've broken the rules, Andy.'

He lifted her off his chest and sat her up. 'What rules?'

'The ones that say lesbians don't have kids.'

'Oh Cass, there are no rules, honey. There's just prejudice and love.' He drew her back towards him. 'And a lot of happy kids with lesbian mums.'

She looked into his face. 'So you don't think it's my fault?'

'God, no.' He squeezed her tight. 'It's nobody's fault. We all wanted this baby, Anna most of all. And we are family now. Anna's going to have her baby tonight and we are going to live happily ever after. Believe me, Cass. I just know it.'

Cass tried to smile. 'I'm just so scared.'

Ruby took her hand. 'Of course you are, darling. We all are.' She glanced at Johnnie. 'We're all scared of losing the people we love most.'

'I can't live without her, Ruby.'

'I know.'

The doctor was at the door. He was older than the last one and tired-looking.

'Which of you are Cass and Andrew?'

Ruby got up to let him sit next to them and his eyes smiled at her through half-moon glasses.

He perched next to Cass.

'Cass, Andrew.' He nodded a greeting. 'I am Mr Singh, the surgeon who performed the operation on your friend Anna.'

Johnnie stood next to Ruby and put his arm around her waist. She squeezed his hand.

'I am pleased to tell you that everything went very well for Anna in theatre. She is through the worst now and is sleeping. She needs rest, but she'll be fine.' He paused as Cass wiped the tears from her face with her coat sleeve. 'You got her to us just in time, young lady. In cases like this, five minutes can make all the difference.'

Cass was shaking with sobs. She held Andy's hand. Everyone was crying with relief. Mr Singh stood up, nodding at them, and smiling.

'And now let me say my congratulations. Your baby has not been at all affected by the unfortunate manner of her birth. You have a lovely baby girl.'

Cass, overcome with gratitude, wrapped her arms around him. 'Thank you, oh thank you. I can never repay you for what you've done for us.'

'No payment necessary, young lady. That is down to the NHS.' He removed her arms from his neck. 'But thank you for the kind thought.'

He walked to the door. 'A nurse will come soon. She will take you to your baby.'

'And Anna?'

'Tomorrow.' He left, bowing at them from the door. 'You may see her tomorrow.'

Chapter 28

Florence Ruth

'Oh, Anna, she's so... she's just...' Greg stroked baby Florence's cheek as she lay asleep in the crib. 'She's beautiful.'

Anna smiled. 'She's a week old today.'

Ruby leant over the bed, across Anna's feet. 'It's those little sideburns that I love. I didn't know babies did Elvis impressions.'

Anna slapped her away. 'It's just a bit of baby hair because she was born early. I told you that yesterday.'

Greg had a tear in his eye. 'She's wonderful, Anna. She looks just like you.'

'Except for the sideburns.' Ruby and Cass laughed. Anna ignored them. She took Greg's hand and he sat on the edge of the bed.

'How are you now, Anna? We were so worried about you.'

'Better. A hell of a lot better for seeing visitors. Except Ruby of course.' Ruby winked at her, eating another of her chocolates. 'I can't wait to get out of this place and go home. Show Florrie her new room.'

Greg smiled. 'I've got a little surprise for you at home. A present for you and Cass and Florence. And Andy too of course, when he's at your house.'

'Oh, Greg, how sweet. What is it?'

'Well, I couldn't bring it in, so I've brought a photo for you.' He gave her a polaroid. 'It's a rocking chair. I've been making it for months. I thought Florence might like being rocked to sleep.'

'Oh, Greg. I don't know what to say.' Anna gazed at the picture. 'It's beautiful. You must have worked so hard on it.' She leant over to kiss him. 'It's the best present I've ever had. Thank you.' They were both tearful. Greg pulled away, embarrassed. 'And Cori wanted me to give the baby this.' He pulled a tiny plastic doll from his jeans pocket. 'Apparently it's Barbie's baby or cousin or something. I know Florrie can't really have it now, but Cori is so excited about you two having a baby.'

'That's so sweet. Tell her Florrie loves it.'

Cass took it from him. 'Ahh, isn't Cori a sweetie! I think her and Florrie are going to be great mates. Look, Ruby.'

Ruby stared at it. 'Absolutely fabulous. Now, Greg, we've done presents, I think it's time to tell your news.'

Greg blushed. 'What news?'

Ruby raised her eyebrows. 'What news, he says. You know what kind of news we girls like. Romance.'

Cass pounced on him. 'Romance? Who with?'

Anna smiled. 'I know. It's Shirley, isn't it?' Greg nodded, looking pleased with himself. 'I'm really happy for you. It's about time you met someone nice.'

Cass laughed. 'And what's Pearl had to say about it?'

'We haven't told her yet. I thought I'd talk to you about it, Cass, because Shirley's still not really speaking to her.'

'God, tell Shirley to give her a break. Pearl's all right.'

'Shirley can't keep punishing Pearl for leaving that prick she was married to.' Ruby was absent-mindedly fiddling with Barbie's baby. 'He was having a fucking affair.'

Anna's mouth dropped. Cass stared at her. 'How do you know that?'

'She got stoned with me and Johnnie a few months ago. Told us all about it.'

Greg was confused. 'But Shirley's never told me that.'

'I don't think she knows. Pearl's probably protecting her from the truth.'

'Poor Pearl.' Anna gazed at Florrie, stroking her cheek. 'She must be really upset if Shirley won't talk to her.'

Ruby smiled at Anna and glanced into the crib. Florence was pressing her hands up to her face in her sleep. 'Anyway, look at little Flo, she doesn't want to hear the sordid truth about adult relationships. She's got years to find that out. What else shall we talk about?' She tapped her finger on her chin, musing. 'I know, let's have a look at your cards.' She leant over to the packed bedside table and picked up a flowery mother and baby scene. 'God, "all our love Auntie Ida and Uncle Sidney (Prestwick)". Frightening! They'll be offering to wash the nappies next.'

Cass spluttered into her coke. Anna frowned. 'Bad taste, Ruby!'

'Sorry.' She smiled at Cass. 'Who else is here then? What's this?' She pulled out a roll of parchment.

Anna took it from her. 'It's Florrie's birth chart. Sky did it for her.'

Cass rolled her eyes at Ruby, who suppressed a smile. Anna saw them.

'Look, if you two are just going to take the piss.'

'No, honestly, I'm just interested. So these must be from your mum, then, Anna.' Ruby had found a collection of crocheted booties stuffed in a plastic bag.

'Right, that's it, Ruby. I'm clearing them away.'

'I'm only teasing! Anyway, I've also got a little present for you all.'

'Oh, Ruby, you needn't have.'

'But I wanted to.' She turned to face the door. 'Andy's setting it up now. He should be in with it soon. Hold on.' She poked her head out of the door. 'I'll be back in a minute.'

As soon as she was gone, Anna turned to Greg. 'So Greg, tell us what's happening with Ruby and Johnnie? Are they back together?'

Greg shrugged. 'Well, he's certainly cheered up. So something must be going on.'

'So have you seen them together?'

'Um, yes, a couple of times, I think.'

'Where were they?'

'I . . .'

'What were they doing?'

'What was she wearing?'

'Er . . .'

'Is he staying the night with her?'

'I don't know, I . . .'

'Has he said anything to you?'

'Has she?'

The doors opened. Ruby was standing there. 'Okay, smile everyone.' Andy came in behind her filming them all with a camcorder. 'You're on *Candid Camera*.'

'Oh my God!' Anna put her hands to her face, laughing. 'You can't give us that, Ruby.'

'Of course I can, and anyway, I have. I want hours of footage of this little Elvis, and I want you all to remember just how happy and gorgeous you all are.'

'Oh Ruby!' Anna squeezed her. 'You're wonderful. Thank you.'

'Hold it.' Andy zoomed in with the camera. 'You two are made for the movies. That's it, if Cass can just move in more to the left. Super. I'm in heaven, I feel like a French *auteur*.' He zoomed into Greg's nostril. 'We could be on *Good Morning Hospital* with Richard and Judy.'

Cass called out. 'Get Florrie, Andy, she's waking up.'

He turned the camera around and focused on the little figure wrapped in a yellow fluffy blanket. Florence Ruth snuffled, rubbing her face with tiny fists. Then she opened her bright blue eyes and stared at the marvelling faces around her.